Tales Over Time

I0548945

Author's website: yesterplace.com

ISBN-13: 978-1-7334044-3-3
ISBN-10: 1-7334044-3-0

First printing: July 2020

The Star Child supreme-hero symbol (page 109) was created by Pat Blanks

Cover artwork/photograph by Greg Rakozy (gregrakozy.com)

Cover design by ThomasMax

Published by:

tm

ThomasMax Publishing
P.O. Box 250054
Atlanta, GA 30325

Praise for Tales Over Time

Tales Over Time is a collection of stories imbued with the true essence of the South and Southern life, by an author who has obviously spent time observing and recording that life. Themes range from 'best laid plans don't always work out' to 'love isn't just a human trait' to 'value isn't the same as worth'. If you love to read true stories of the real South—and as every Southerner knows, truth is often, if not always, in the eye of the beholder—then these are the stories for you.

  – K.G. McAbee, Author of numerous short stories and several books, Artist in Residence with South Carolina Arts Commission. https://www.kgmcabeebooks.com/

The characters that populate Susan Lindsley's collection of short stories display human frailties we can recognize, laugh at, and forgive. These folksy tales are a delight to read.

  -- Marcia Preston (M. K. Preston) author of *The Spiderling* 2020).
www.marciapreston.com

Short stories are an art form that the average writer rarely masters. The ability to take a snippet of life, honing in on details, and taking a small part of living and making it a tale. Susan Lindsley shows us that art in her stories, with a talent that subtly draws you in. I read short stories one or two at a time, then put the book down to digest what I just read. It's a treat the next day picking up the book again and seeing what treasure I find, knowing it will be different from the night before, but the voice will be consistently reliable in its pleasure. Lindsley's stories have an everyday-feel about them, but by the end you realize she has a skill in how she interprets the world.

  –C. Hope Clark, author of the award-winning Carolina Slade Mysteries and the Edisto Island Mysteries. www.chopeclark.com

AWARD WINNING STORIES

Susan Lindsley has won numerous awards for her writings over the years. Several stories in this collection have been honored:

The Mason Jar (page 10), Third Place, The Vega Award for Speculative Fiction, The Southeastern Writers Association, 2020

Robbie and a Car Named Bradley (page 14), Winner, Microcosm Award, Southeastern Writers Conference, 2019; Second Place, The Youth/Adult/Middle grade Award, The Southeastern Writers Association, 2020.

How to (Not) Deer Hunt (page 31) Second Place, Short Fiction, Southeastern Writers Conference, 2019

The Old Lady and the Wooden Spools (page 49), Third Place, The George Thomas Youngblood Award for Short Story, The Southeastern Writers Association, 2020

Judge Stone and the Moonshiners (page 52), Winner, The George Thomas Youngblood Award, Southeastern Writers Conference, 2019

A Saturday Afternoon in Georgia (page 77), Winner, Historical Fiction Award, Southeastern Writers Association, 2020

Return from the Undiscovered Country (page 90), Winner, the Vega Award, Southeastern Writers Conference, 2019

Flower of the Fleet (page 110), Winner, Humor Award, Southeastern Writers Association, 2020

Tales Over Time

Susan Lindsley

ThomasMax

Your Publisher
For The 21st Century

The Virus

We are all in this together
So they say,
And we are
Until I catch Corona,
For then I am alone
In quarantine
No one to hold my hand
Or say "I love you"
Or "Goodbye."
No one to twine
A loving finger in my own,

Just isolation
And the ghostly creatures
Clad like aliens
Who tread on whispered soles
To change my tubes,
To add more air
Or fluid
Or take away my waste.

We are together
As I die
Alone
But for the nurse
So kind to me just yesterday
Who sleeps beyond my reach
As she lies dying too,
Six feet apart,
Together.

In memory of those who have gone,

With respect for all who provided medical care

With thanks to those who supported the medical teams

ACKNOWLEDGMENTS

I wish to thank Pat Blanks, fellow student and lifelong friend, for her eagle eye in proofing and providing a tough editing-read of the manuscript, story-by-story.

The cover picture was taken by Greg Rakozy who graciously gave me permission to use it. Thanks, Greg.

I cannot say "thank you" enough to the three people who reviewed the manuscript and provided quotes to support my work: Marcia Preston, Hope Clark, and K.G. McAbee.

As she has for a quarter century, my life partner Gail Cabisius has given me and my work unconditional support in many ways.

Thank you, Lee Clevenger, who worked so hard to get this book into print so quickly. It is dear to me because of the viral plague and my desire to recognize it and to express my thanks to those who stand in the front lines for us all.

TABLE OF CONTENTS

OTHER BOOKS BY SUSAN LINDSLEY

Southern historical novels
    The Bottom Rail
    When Darkness Fell

Memoirs
    Blue Jeans and Pantaloons in YESTERPLACE
    Possum Cops, Poachers and the Counterfeit Game Warden

Biography: The Lindsleys of Westover
              Susan Myrick of Gone With The Wind:
                    An Autobiographical Biography

Collections of works edited
    Myrick Memories
    Margaret Mitchell: A Scarlett or a Melanie?
    Luther Lindsley: His Literary Works

Poetry
    When Yestertime Was Now
    Christmas Gift
    O Yesterplace and other poems (out of print)

Short Story collections
    Finding Bigfoot
    Whitetails and Tall Tales
    Emperor of the United American States

Wildlife
    Wildlife in Persimmon Paradise

DVD: MYRICK DISCUSSES PEGGY and GWTW

FACING COVID-19

Peggy knew she would be the topic of conversation if she did not go to the funeral. She was probably already the talk of the plant since she had not shown up for work today.   Jackson had been her supervisor and friend at the plant for more than twenty years, since she had been promoted from the typing pool to secretary and then on to administrative assistant to the plant manager.

But she had no intention of going to the funeral and catching whatever it was that seemed to be killing off people not just across the States but all over the world. Something that looked like a basketball with lots of funny looking stuff poking out of it.

If you have some pre-existing ailment, the TV people warned you, and you catch this thing, you may as well write yourself off. Her cousin had called last week and told her about a neighbor who had felt bad on Friday, gone to the emergency room and was dead on Monday because she had asthma. The infection delighted in joining up with another ailment to kill off people like her who had what the experts were calling pre-existing conditions.

Peggy had had a heart attack four years ago, and, thank the Lord, the four stents Dr. Bonner had put into her system had kept her going, but not going on all eight cylinders as she could before. And even worse, he told her she had a myxoma growing on the wall of her heart. So she had two threats to start with: A bunch of stents and a funny little tumor. No way was she going to lay out the welcome mat for the basketball with golf tees growing from it.

She was going to retire. Right now. Let them bury Jackson without her in sight and when they returned to the plant, they would learn they had seen the last of her—she would be gone on vacation and retired.

She would attend the burial, but not to mingle and collect a share of that virus. She would stand on the upper edge of the cemetery near the woods to watch. On the dirt road used mostly by the cemetery workers, where she would have a good view of Jackson's family plot. She could see but not be noticed. No way was she going to be a statistic like those idiots down in South Georgia who went to a funeral and about two weeks later seemed like the whole town started coming down with the bug. More than a hundred dead. Nope, she was not going to be a statistic related to someone else's funeral, even as much as she owed to Jackson.

Some hospitals were full. She had heard that some patients lay in beds in the hallways. There were not enough breathing machines in the state to supply what the local hospital was going to need once those idiots got Jackson buried and the bug really hit the hundred-fifty-plus people who hugged and whispered and carried on at the funeral parlor.

Even the men who stood on the porch to smoke away the visiting hours could succumb, their demise maybe helped along by all that smoke.

She took a deep breath, let it out, and picked up her cell phone. Pushed the buttons for Emily in personnel at the plant. Emily's phone would show who called, but would not show if she were at home or still on the road.

"Emily, it's Peggy."

"Where are you? Are you okay?"

"Yes, I'm fine. I know this is sudden, but I need to take that vacation I've put off for years. As of today. I have the time coming. I've always wanted to go to Africa on safari and I'm going now." She glanced at the Road Scholar's flyer and read a few words to Emily.

"Vacation? You? Isn't it a bad time? What about…I mean, with us losing Mr. Jackson and you next in line for manager…" Her voice trailed off.

"I just have to take this trip, Emily. I may not get another chance for this and it's been my dream. And I think it's time I retired. A two-week vacation, and then retirement. That'll give me full pay for two weeks and then I can get my social security plus company retirement and my Roth, and I'll be able to …." She paused. She didn't want to say "survive," although that word fit. Survival was her goal now, survival away from people.

"Well, you know. I'm just ready. Losing Mr. Jackson's been a blow and I don't want to take on that load at my age. Please just get the paperwork done. And I'll be back in town in two weeks and in touch."

"Won't you be at the funeral? Aren't you back in town? Maybe we could sit together."

"What? Oh, yes. Of course. I'll look for you. I'll be in touch."

Peggy disconnected. She never said goodbye on the phone, but ended any conversation when she was ready by clicking off. She had no intention of looking for Emily or sitting with anyone. Cousin Ed up in Seattle said this flu was the worse he'd heard of, even killing a bunch of old folks in a nursing home and nobody knew what to do to treat them. Ed said he was taking a vacation in his Winnebago and getting out of town before one of the aides at the nursing home brought that flu into his neighborhood.

She settled into her recliner, pulled a lap board across her legs, and began listing the items she would need for a long stay in the house. She was going to outlast the bug if it came to town.

She called the pharmacists at Walgreens and told them she was going out of the country for a month and needed to get all her meds renewed even if the insurance would not pay. She would have to have them all for thirty days. And she would pay the extra.

Two hours later, she was in the Publix three miles from home. Not the one three blocks away, where the employees knew her and hugged her each time she shopped. Not today. Suppose one of them had the virus already. No one paid her any mind at the more distant store. But when she pushed her cart to checkout, the clerk looked at her purchases and grinned, "Looks like you're planning a long stay somewhere."

"Yes, well, you know how it is when you have a lot of company for two weeks. Got to be prepared for anything." She placed two giant packs of Charmin Gentle on the checkout belt and said, "One of my guests has a problem. I had to get two, but they are the last two packages on the shelf."

"Oh my, I understand," the clerk said. "I've been there myself. Don't worry. The truck comes in tomorrow."

As she rolled her cart to the parking lot, she overhead an incoming customer say, "Must going to be a shortage of toilet paper. I better stock up too."

At home, Peggy unloaded her Publix supplies and headed for Walgreens to collect her prescriptions.

On the way in she passed the paper stocks, thought, "What the heck," and threw in two packs of toilet paper. She turned down the junk food aisle and grabbed two family packs of M & Ms.

At the pharmacy she found the meds she was most worried about: Lumigan for her glaucoma and Lovastatin for her cholesterol. And the nitroglycerin for just-in- case. She hadn't needed the nitro since the heart attack, but decided if she was going to stay inside for a month, or however long, she might want it. The bottle in the cabinet expired two years ago. No way would she go to the doctor or hospital with this virus raging over everything.

The clerk said, "I understand you're going out of the country. Are you worried about that new virus going around?"

"No. I'll be on vacation and will be on a safari in South Africa. I don't imagine there'll be any problems there. I can always come home if I need to."

"We're closing for the funeral in just another hour. I'm glad you got here in time. I reckon I'll see you at the funeral."

"Most likely," Peggy said, paid the extra for getting the prescription early and headed to her car, grateful to get out without further talk of the funeral. It was so hard to keep the truth from all these people who knew her and where she worked and even knew when her dog died and who cleaned her house.

The thought reminded her that she would have to call Sherry and tell her not to come clean next week.

Peggy put away her purchases, ate a late lunch, and dressed for the funeral. A dark pants suit, low-heel black shoes with anklet hose. She put on light makeup, gathered up purse and keys and drove to the cemetery.

No cars. The tent was set up over the open grave. Peggy took the dirt road that circled the cemetery and drove to the top of the ridge overlooking the entire hundred acres. She parked in the shade of a white oak where she would have a perfect view through the passenger side window of the burial services when they began. She could step out and watch from behind the car and not be seen if she wanted to. She checked the time. The church service should be ending about now and the crowd would take another thirty minutes or longer to reach the cemetery. She spent the time on her cell phone, researching the virus.

Everywhere she looked on the web she saw plenty of reasons to be afraid and to be ready to hide away in her home without any visitors. Let them think she was on a trip to Africa.

It would be hot over there, as it was getting hot here in the car. She cranked it and touched the window beside her. It felt hot. She ran the windows down and switched off the engine. Just in time to have silence on the hill as the hearse arrived with a mile-long line of cars following it.

She turned off her phone, dropped it on the passenger seat and decided to step outside.

As she did so, a squirrel barked at her, flipped his tail and scampered up the oak. A jay squawked. She ignored the wood sounds, something moving the dry leaves, the breeze pushing the last of the white oak leaves free to slide down. A rattling noise. She shifted weight onto her left leg and moved her right one a bit toward the front of the car. Something slammed fire and pain into the calf of her right leg.

She screamed and jerked her leg up. The rattler struck again, injected a dose into her other leg and fled.

No one heard her scream. She sank to the ground with the pain and realized she either had to get up and drive to get help or she would die.

She crawled into the car. Once behind the wheel, she lay both hands palm down on the steering wheel and her face on her hands. Sweats and chills began. She recognized the heart attack only seconds before she died.

The Korona Brothers remind you

*Wash your hands
*Wear your mask
*Keep a safe distance

A CLOSE ENCOUNTER

"You be good now, Harry," Mama said. "Remember to do whatever Myrtle tells you to. I'll be back to fix your supper." She reached down to her three-year-old and hugged him. "Love you," she said, released her son and headed for the door.

As the door closed, Myrtle strolled into the living room from the kitchen. She held a cup of coffee in one hand and a donut in the other. "You want to play outside?" she asked.

"Can I?" Harrison asked. "And can I have a donut too?"

"Sure," Myrtle said. She led the way to the kitchen. Harrison scrambled into his chair by the breakfast table.

"I want a chocolate one," he said.

"You do want some milk too?"

"Un-huh."

"Doesn't your mother tell you to say 'yes, ma'am?'"

"Yes, ma'am," he said.

"That's better." Myrtle reached into the donut box from Krispy Kreme and lifted out a chocolate-iced crème donut, set it on a saucer, and laid it on the table in front of Harrison. Before she had poured a cup of milk, he had devoured the treat. Icing covered his lips.

She pulled a paper towel from the rack over the sink and wiped his face. "You drink up this here milk," she ordered.

He gulped it down and gave himself a mustache in the process. Again, she wiped his face.

"Let's go outside," she said and opened the sliding door to the back porch. Harrison scampered onto the porch and held onto the railing as he eased himself to the ground. Myrtle settled her bulk onto the swing, which faced the back yard. "Don't you runoff, now, you hear?"

"Yes, ma'am," he said. He loped down on the sandpile and began loading his red dump truck with sand.

Moments later, Myrtle made a sound he didn't understand and he looked toward the porch. She lay on her side in the swing, with her feet on the floor. He returned to his dump truck. Myrtle was taking a nap.

Two hours later, he crawled up onto the porch. "I'm hungry," he said and shook Myrtle's shoulder. She did not move, but stared at him. She didn't blink. "Don't be mad at me. I'm just hungry. Ma'am."

No answer.

He went into the kitchen and found the donut box. It contained three donuts. In less than three minutes, he had stuffed them down. He pulled open the Frigidaire and tried to lift the half gallon of milk. He struggled with its weight but couldn't hold it. The jug slammed to the floor and the loose cap popped off. Milk ran over the floor.

"Myrtle," he yelled and ran onto the porch. He shook her shoulder. She did not move.

"Mama's gone be mad at me," he whispered. "Please, wake up."

She did not move.

He scampered down the steps, stumbled and fell from the bottom step. He scrambled to his feet and ran across the yard, fearing Myrtle's anger. She had scolded him often and once had smacked his bottom.

At the edge of the yard, he hesitated only long enough to look back and see Myrtle still sleeping on the swing. He darted into the shadows of the woods and kept moving away from punishment.

With the family home on the edge of the national forest, he faced miles of woods. Paths worn by wildlife led him deeper and closer to safety from the anger that lay behind him. Shadows seemed to move toward him. Silence lay ahead and noises rose behind him.

Unaware of time or distance, he kept going, taking a path here, another there. Up a hill to another path that circled to his right. Then a fork, going downhill where he faced a stream. He walked to the rocks on the edge and watched the water whiten at it tumbled over large stones. Minnows darted away from his reflection. He saw a spring lizard in the still shallows and reached for it, but the animal scurried away ahead of his grasp.

He lifted a small rock smoothed by years of tumbling in the stream bed, and threw it toward the rapids. The splash was lost in the whitewater. He threw another one. And suddenly plopped down.

He needed to go to the bathroom. Mama would fuss if he didn't use the toilet, but he had to go NOW. He looked around to see who might be watching, but the woods held only a squirrel barking from an oak limb. He knew Mama would be proud after he urinated and didn't go on himself. Except for a few drops on his hand. He wiped the hand on the seat of his pants.

"I'm hungry," he muttered. "Myrtle, where are you?"

He turned around to go home. Two paths lured him with the promise of home. But which one? He started up one, went a few yards, stopped at a fork.

Harrison realized he did not know how to get home. He sat down and began to cry. He knuckled at his eyes as the sobs shook his entire body. The sun was falling behind the distant hills and the night chill was coming. Cold joined his fear in making him shake.

Something rustled leaves a little way up the path. He thought it was a squirrel until he glanced up to see a bear standing on her hind legs. "A mama," he said as he saw its breasts and realized it didn't have the same things he and daddy had. He pushed himself up onto his hands and feet, and then upright, and staggered toward the mama.

She stood and watched. The boy wrapped his arms around her leg and looked up. She smiled, reached down, placed her hands under his armpits and lifted him the way his mother did. The animal set him on one forearm and used her other furry hand to coax Harry to lay his head against her chest. He closed his eyes and drifted to sleep as her body heat and fur warmed him and eased his fear. She carried him deep into the woods.

At a patch of blackberries, she stopped and stood Harry down. She grunted and nibbled at some blackberries. Harrison stuck his face against a stem and nibbled at one, only to jerk his face back as a briar stuck his skin. He backed away from the berries.

The animal lifted him again, stood upright and carried Harrison farther along the path. When she smelled his need to defecate, she placed him on the ground and watched as he pulled down his pants, squatted and dumped. She pulled a few leaves from a mulberry tree and wiped his bottom. Darkness fell and she continued to a cave where she cradled him while he slept through the night.

Morning brought the distant music of a hound on a trail. Harrison slept on. The animal lifted the sleeping child, cradled him close to her chest, and backtracked toward the baying hound. When she reached the creek, she laid him in the warmth of the early sun. She slipped a few yards into the woods and watched.

Harrison woke, alone and hungry. He looked around for his bear, and spotted her off in the woods. The dog came closer and he heard his father's voice calling his name. He got to his feet as the dog charged from the woods, spotted the boy, and leaped up to lick his face. Boy and dog tumbled to the ground. Harrison hollered with delight.

Daddy arrived and lifted his son. Harrison wiggled in his father's arms, repeated "Look it, look it," and pointed to the woods. Daddy looked in time to catch a glimpse of Bigfoot as she lumbered away into the morning.

THE MASON JAR

I am Mason Jar. I came to Tickleboro in a box with a lot of my kin. They are gone now, but a lot more kin have come to replace them. I am old and have been into a lot of hot water. I held homemade blackberry jam, green beans, butter beans, and tomatoes at different times. I spent a lot of winters on narrow wooden shelves in a smoke house where hams hung from the ceiling and wood and coals filled the house with smoke.

I have heard people speak, and wish I could talk back to them. But the people are gone away and I have been wrapped up with paper and piled into a box with a lot of other quart jars. I don't like being stuffed inside a box. I cannot do anyone any account if I'm stuck in a box. I can't hold fruit, I can't show off the colors of the tomatoes or the translucence of sweet cucumber pickles if I am hauled off from this home, away from its garden that has given me so much to hold inside over the fall and through the coldest times.

Oh, someone is opening up the box. He is skinny. Not rotund like the farmers.

But I have seen him. He and his wife Esther came to Ellen and Homer's house for supper one night and I saw him from where I sat on the kitchen shelf. His wife Esther fussed at Jerry when he took another jar—not a Mason jar, but some short of flat one, out of a paper sack and offered it to Homer. I don't know what was in that bottle, but it was clear, and after they all drank it, they laughed and giggled a lot. Esther didn't drink any of it—she said something about she had to drive him home.

Skinny Jerry holds me up to the light. "This here one is like I remember from when Ma pickled peaches," he said. "I ain't seen one this old since afore we started running shine. I especially like it being blue."

Another man laughed. He was fat. Both of them had on dirty overalls. And inside a house. Farmers I knew weren't let in the kitchen if they had on dirty overalls. The farmers' wives, even before Ellen, who filled me up every summer never wore dirty clothes. The ladies never wore overalls anyhow, but dresses I heard one of them say were made out of feed sacks. Some had colors like I got to hold. Reds, greens, yellow. Only my being blue made the colors inside me look different to people.

Skinny said, "Well, old or not, all these here jars are perfect fer our 'shine. Right size, and we can get caps easy at the grocery. Put this here box in the truck. In the cab. We don't want hit sliding all over the bed and busting up them jars."

I was stuffed back into the box, into the darkness. I got left there for a long time, and was so glad when the box was put down and Skinny Jerry opened the top. I felt the warm sunlight. It wasn't as warm as the pot when the farmer's wife cooked up her food in the pressure cooker with me and another bunch of Mason Jars, but it was bright, not dark like the inside of the cooker.

Jerry poked around in the box and said, "Looks like they all made it. None's broke."

He walked away. The sun moved away too. Came back and went away. Rain came, and some ran into my insides. It felt cold. I wasn't used to cold. The box began to fall apart, and all of us pushed to get out. I lay on some moss, but some rolled away. I heard one scream as it hit a rock and busted wide open. I didn't want to roll into a rock. I wanted to be filled up again, to feel my inside full of warmth from food or pickles.

Jerry yelled, "Hell, Jack, you done left the box of jars out to get wet. We done lost one what rolled onto a rock."

"I should-a put that-air table cloth over it."

"Under hit too. Well, can't do nuthin' bout it now. You got them lids?"

"Shore."

"Well, let's get to filling these here jars."

"What about the water in 'em?"

"That ain't gonna hurt nothing. We'll just pore it out. The hooch'll kill anything in the jar."

My turn came. Skinny turned me upside down to pour out the rain water and the three leaves that had fallen inside. Then he poured something that looked as clear as spring water—I know about spring water because I was once the jar the men used to drink from when they broke from hauling hay in the hot days. I was lucky I wasn't broken and Ellen found me and took me back to hold her canning.

Skinny filled me up and handed me to the Fat Man. He tightened a lid on and put me into a divided box. I couldn't feel the others as they got shoved into a small compartment.

Fat Man asked, "Since Pickens is outta jail from rustling, we gonna keep him in the loop?"

"Yeah. He's looking for two boxes tonight. You want to take those and I'll keep on filling the rest of the jars? Come back and don't forget to get the money."

I couldn't hear anything else for the longest time except for rattling from the truck. The road must have been dirt cause the truck bounced and groaned and I felt scared I might get busted. But it finally stopped. Fat Man jostled the box as he toted it to the door.

"Hey, Pickens," he yelled. "Got your hooch."

Pickens toted the box inside, opened the top, and pulled out one of my clear-sided cousins. He unscrewed the lid and tipped the jar to his mouth, swallowed, screwed the lid back on, set the jar down, wiped his mouth with the back of his hand, and said, "You make it as good as you did before I went to jail. I kin buy all you make. I got a buyer all set."

Fat man laughed. "Bet I know who."

"Yep, same as before I went to Jackson. He said he was tired of having to go to Milledgeville to get his hooch."

"I kin bring you more soon's it runs off. We got one other customer, but he don't want much."

Pickens closed up the box and I couldn't hear them good. Seemed like they left the room. Next thing was getting moved into a car, going somewhere and then Pickens took me into another house.

"Hey, Commissioner Stevens," he said. "Here's two dozen jars. They keep you a few days? They gonna have a full run by tomorrow. I can get it to you the next day."

Commissioner? I wondered. I didn't have long to wonder. He opened up my box and tasted from another jar. "Damn spanking good," he said. "I can use about a hundred jars a week if your men can supply that much. I'm sick and tired of having to pay a driver to go to Milledgeville every week."

I knew him too, from when he was the chairman of the Tickle-boro County commissioners. He had been to parties over at Ellen's when he was running for office and Ellen's husband was on his committee to help him get elected.

Pickens laughed. "I'll get the word back. They might need a money boost to get up to that level. And some protection from the law."

"Tell them not to worry about the law. I'll arrange for the sheriff to stay away. They'll need to give him say a dozen pints a week is all. And Judge Shep is one of my friends..."

Pickens snickered. "Yeah, he had me run him two dozen bottles for one of his parties. I know he ain't gonna jail any of us even if the revenuers come down here."

"Here's your money," the commissioner said.

Pickens hadn't been gone long enough to drive back to his house when someone knocked on the door. Commissioner let someone in who entered the room where I was in my box.

"Here's two dozen jars," the commissioner said. "Tell Senator Murray more's coming tomorrow. I have a local producer now, so we can schedule delivery better."

I was carried somewhere again, only this time the vehicle wasn't a rattle-trap truck. I felt I was being carried on air. But we all got juggled when the man toted us up the steps to a high floor. Maybe up two flights or maybe three.

I have never seen such a room. Red curtains, red sofas, women wearing almost nothing, the air so thick I thought the smoke was going to fall through the lid when one of the men took my top off. He held me out to one of the half-naked women. "Have a taste of this, sugar plum," he said.

She replied, "I may be a whore, but I don't drink moonshine out of a Mason Jar any more than your wife does. Get me a glass."

He slapped her.

"That's how you treat your wife?" She grabbed me from his hand, slung the whiskey into his face, and threw me to the wall.

I B U S T E D.

ROBBIE AND A CAR NAMED BRADLEY

As Bradley the BMW purred along toward home, Robbie glanced down to his cell phone as he texted. He paid no heed to noise or the pull and wobble of the steering wheel. Katie had let him kiss her goodnight for the first time and he had to boast to his football buddy.

The noise rose into a rhythm and Bradley headed for the ditch on the left side of the road.

An approaching driver gave him an *I-find-you-disgusting* finger as he swerved almost into the ditch to avoid a crash. Robbie jerked on the wheel, but the thumping got louder. Robbie wrestled the steering wheel until he was able to get Bradley back onto his side of the road, pulled onto the shoulder and stopped.

He whooshed. He had not wrecked, and he didn't want to go to Georgia Tech without a car. He needed Bradley if he was going to visit Katie across the metro area at Agnes Scott and not have to change buses every few blocks. Besides, you can't count on the Metro.

"Oh, Bradley," he whispered, "what's the matter with you?"

He looked for his cell phone. It had bounced to the floorboards during his struggle. It was still on, his text message to his football-team buddy unfinished and not sent. He finished the sentence and added, "Bradley has died on me. I don't know what to do."

The buddy replied, "Where are you? Why don't you call your father?"

"He's at work."

"What happened?"

"I don't know. Bradley made a god-awful thumping noise and pulled himself into the other lane. I nearly got creamed by another car. I had to use both hands to get Bradley back on my side and off the road. And he really bumped, like last weekend on that back road full of potholes."

"Maybe you could look it over and figure out what's wrong."

"Me look it over? Man, I don't know anything about cars except how to not get caught by the cops when I speed." He chuckled. "Or how to talk myself out of a ticket."

"Well, take a look anyhow."

"Okay."

He shoved the phone into his pocket, opened the door and was greeted by the blaring horn of a car as it swerved to avoid hitting the door. He looked back and waited for two more cars to pass before he jumped out, slammed the door and ran around the front end of the car.

He saw the flat tire.

Now what?

He looked up at traffic, shook his head, crawled in the passenger-side door, sat and pulled out his phone to call his father.

The secretary answered. Robbie said, "I need to talk to my dad."

"He's in a meeting with his attorney and said not to disturb him for anything other than a dire family emergency."

"Well, this is a dire emergency. I need to talk to him."

He heard the *Blue Danube Waltz* begin as she put him on hold. Moments later, "What is it, Robbie?" His father sounded gruff.

"I'm out on 212 and have a flat tire and nearly got in a wreck and I don't know what to do."

"You change it, Robbie. A flat tire is not an emergency. Change the tire." Dad hung up.

Robbie almost screamed as he asked the phone, "How, Daddy? How?"

He pounded his forehead on the dashboard four times and jerked himself upright. "Billy. He'll know what to do." Billy was the country-boy captain of the high school football team. He knew all about mechanical things like cars and tractors.

He texted Billy, who gave him instructions: "Look in the trunk, Stupid. You've got a jack, a lug wrench and a spare tire. Jack up the car, undo the lugs, and put on the spare."

Oh gad, what in blazes are those? I can't ask him what are a lug wrench and a lug. And what's a jack anyhow?

Robbie sat for several minutes while he considered his options. He couldn't call Daddy again. He didn't dare let Billy know he had no idea what those things were. He pulled out his wallet and looked at the few bills. Eighteen dollars would not pay for a wrecker. Maybe they would take his credit card.

He searched on his smart phone, found a wrecker service nearby and called.

"I need a wrecker. My car just died on me. I don't know what's the matter. I lost control of the steering. I'm parked on the shoulder."

The dispatcher, a soft-voiced lady, said she would send help right away, a wrecker was available.

"I don't have much cash. Will you take a credit card?" She would, but needed the card number. He was happy to give it and gritted his teeth as he hoped Daddy wouldn't go over the bills too closely.

While he waited for the wrecker, Robbie paced along the street, moving behind the car when he saw lights approaching. He was going to be late calling Katie to say goodnight. *I hope she's not worried but I'm not going to call her and tell her I have a flat tire.*

He thought about tomorrow night, the high school prom, and the weekend he'd been looking forward to for weeks since Katie agreed to go with him. And Monday afternoon, graduation, valedictorian. He grinned and boxed the air. Four-point-oh, highest grade average ever in the high school and a full scholarship to Georgia Tech.

Katie had been impressed when he told her of the scholarship. She had earned hers to Agnes Scott.

Headlights approached, but not from Macon. The vehicle rattled, and when he turned to see who it might be, bright lights came on and the pickup slowed, drew alongside him, and the window came down.

"You got troubles, boy?" the man asked.

Robbie shook inside as he saw the grubby unshaven face, the oil-stained cap, and the snaggled teeth, two incisors missing. The hand hanging outside the window was dirty, the fingers pointed to the car.

"That-air BMW looks new, boy. It ought not be no trouble. Let me take a look-see."

The man stepped out and the driver came around. The passenger went to the hood, but Robbie said, "It's a flat tire. I have somebody coming to help me."

"Flat tire? You got a flat tire is all?" Both men laughed.

The driver said, "If you got a flat tire and gonna pay somebody to fix it cause you might git that-air fancy suit dirty, you can pay us."

"I got a friend coming," Robbie replied.

"Yeah? Well how about you just pay us not to whup you and take the money anyhow?"

The man stepped close and leaned his face inches from Robbie's. "You got money, ain'tcha, boy? How's about you jest reach in that-air back pocket and take out that billfold and hand it over?"

Robbie's gut twisted. "I don't have any…"

"Give me that billfold or I'll knock out your two front teeth same as mine."

Robbie slipped his left hand behind himself and pulled out his wallet. The man took it, passed it behind himself and said, "Take out his cash and throw it over the hood and we'll leave this fancy stupid-oh to figure out how to change a tire."

Robbie saw his wallet sail over the hood. The man shoved him against the BMW door, stuck a foot behind Robbie's knee and jerked him down.

Laughing, the men scurried into the truck and it roared off. Robbie scrambled to his feet and stared at the tail lights as the truck rounded the curve.

He crawled into the front seat, started the engine, turned on the headlights and got out to search for his wallet. It lay near the flat. He pushed it into his pocket, crawled into the front seat and turned off the lights.

Headlights approached from the direction of Macon. "Oh God, don't let them come back."

Robbie sank down in the seat, but breathed in relief when he realized it was the tow truck. The driver stopped, turned in the road, and backed the tow truck close enough to attach the chains to Bradley. He turned on his spotlight and stepped out of the truck.

Robbie saw an old man in worn, stained jeans, a cheap cotton shirt with sleeves rolled up, and scuffed, oil-spotted boots. Robbie grimaced at the thought of depending on the likes of this ignorant man for help.

As he came toward the disabled car, the man stopped, stared at the flat, and looked up at the worried teenager.

"You just got a flat tire, son. How come you called a tow truck? You could-a saved a heap of money if you just changed it yourself."

Robbie looked at the ground. "I don't know how." His face burned with embarrassment.

The older man shook his head. "I'll show you how to change it. But you'll be charged for a wrecker call." He studied the youth and said, "Ain't you Robbie Benson?"

Robbie nodded.

His lips tucked in, the man shook his head. *Smart as a whip and dumb as a jackass. Not worth a tinker's dam for anything. I got to tell my Katie she can't date him no more.*

CROSSING OTTER CREEK

Behind their backs, other students at the University referred to the two roommates as *Salt* and *Beets* since one of the girls was white and the other a distant descendant of an Indian and other races. From Puerto Rico, Beets tanned to a reddish hue rather than burned when she was in the sun. When the two eventually heard the nicknames they burst into laughter.

Neither had noticed the difference in skin tone in their two-year friendship until they heard their nicknames. Neither cared.

Summers, Beets flew home for the long vacation, but spent the other holidays with Salt and her family in Tickleboro, Georgia. She grew to love the small-town atmosphere and when at graduation, she applied for a job as x-ray technician at the Tickleboro clinic, she was accepted. Salt had already landed a job as history teacher at the local high school and had told Beets she was going to have fun teaching about the Spanish-American War being started by reporters who blew up the Maine.

Beets lived with Salt and her family for a couple of weeks until she found a small one-bedroom house with a fenced yard. She wanted a dog, and Salt's family had two of their own. They said "no more" in their home. When Beets got settled into her own place, she began to look into ads in the paper and those posted on the bulletin board of the local grocery. Might take a while to find what she wanted, but she could be patient.

Ten days later, she saw the ad at the grocery story. "Collie/shepherd mixed pups. Two male, three females. $50.00." It gave an address. Beets did not wait. She pulled her copy of the local county map out of the pocket of the truck, found the street, and off she went in her battered secondhand pickup.

She crossed the river, drove through town, found the dirt-road turnoff, and followed its twists for more than a mile when she spotted the rough-cut slab hand painted with "Otter Creek" and an arrow pointing to her right. She turned right and crossed the one-lane wooden bridge over a rocky stream. Another mile, and she passed a mama-papa style store on her left, with three men leaning against the hood of a Ford Ranger 150 pickup. She smiled and waved and continued on her way through the late morning shadows of white oaks.

What a wonderful place to live. Maybe when I'm older and can save enough money I can buy some land here. I could love these oaks as much as palm trees.

She braked as a gray fox squirrel dashed across the road.

When she glanced in the rearview mirror to see if the squirrel made it across the road, she noticed the truck from the store had followed her. She recognized the three white men from the convenience store by their John Deere caps. The driver and the outside passenger draped an arm through the open windows. Behind them she could see what looked like long guns hanging in front of the rear window. A hound stuck its head over the side and peered down the road toward her, its ears flapping in the wind.

Must be going to hunt rabbits or something. They're going to be as brown as me if they keep their arms out like that in the sun.

They took every turn she did. When she pulled in at the red mailbox painted with 1518, the other truck continued down the dirt road, but its driver gunned the motor and lifted half the dirt from the road into dust that flooded into her vehicle even with the windows closed and the air conditioner running. She coughed. Her eyes stung. She eased up the driveway and tried to blink some of the dust from her eyes.

She pulled up near a doublewide trailer. *Should I get out or honk?* But dogs answered her self-question. Two adults and five puppies charged toward her truck with their tails wagging. Their barking, however, decided her to wait.

The trailer door opened and a blond woman stepped onto the stoop. She wore a cotton housedress and loafers without socks. Beets summed her up. *She needs to comb her hair. And looks like she doesn't even wear a bra. But I'll bet she's cooler than I am in this hot bra and July heat—hotter than back home where at least we mostly had some sort of ocean breeze.*

The woman walked into the yard and hollered. The dogs ran to her. Beets stepped out of the truck and said, "Thanks for calling the dogs. I saw your ad and came to get a puppy."

"You have fifty dollars?"

"I do. Are these the puppies?"

"Yes. Where are you from? I haven't seen you here-abouts before. And you talk funny."

"Over across the river, on the other side of Tickleboro. I'm from Puerto Rico. I've been living here just a little while."

"But you said you have the money to pay for the puppy? You have a job?"

"Oh, yes, Ma'am, I have a job. I work over at the hospital. I am an x-ray technician."

"Okay, take your pick of the puppies."

"These here in the yard? "

"Yep. Any one you want."

She looked them over. They scrapped with each other and took turns rolling across the dusty yard. She whistled. The games ended and the puppies looked around for the source of the whistle. "Here, pup," she called and patted her knee.

The feisty one that had tumbled its sibling ran to her and jumped its front feet onto her thighs.

"I'll take this one," she said and lifted the pup into her arms.

"Pay before you put it in your truck," the woman demanded.

Beets reached into her pocket, removed a folded $50.00 bill and handed it to the woman.

The woman unfolded the bill, held it up for sunlight to bleed through, nodded, and said, "Okay. The dog's yours. You need to leave now."

Beets pushed the pup into the bench seat, scrambled in behind it, and headed home.

At she left the driveway, she noticed the pickup that had followed her as she came for the puppy. It was parked some fifty feet down the road to her right as she turned left. It pulled out behind her.

Must be some friends of hers afraid I might steal one of the puppies, she thought and went her way.

Pup began to pant and drool and push against her. "You want some water, pooch?" she asked. As if it knew what she said, the puppy wagged its tail and tried to crawl into her lap.

"We'll stop at the store up ahead and get some water. I could use some too. But you have to stay in the truck. I don't have a leash and if I let you out, no telling where you might go."

As she approached the store, she noticed two young men leaning on the hood of a brown and tan Chevy pickup and talking to each other over the hood. It made her think of her father back home, the way he chatted with his friends in their yard, all leaning on the hood of a truck. She smiled as she parked, stepped out and waved at the two men.

The Ford pulled into the shade beside the Chevy as she turned toward the store.

Overhead fans *whumped* but only moved hot air around. An old man rose from a stool behind the counter and studied her. She smiled. "I want a couple of bottles of water. My new puppy and I are both thirsty."

He didn't speak, just pointed toward the back of the store. She strode to the cooler, pulled out two bottles of water, and returned to the counter. "Sir, you need to get some of those young men in here to help you out. Let one of them sit in this corner where its hot, and you go sit under the fan. "

"That'll be two dollars and nineteen cents," was his reply.

She handed him three ones, and he counted the change, from two-nineteen up to the three dollars. "Hey, I like that," she said. "Most folks don't know how to count change anymore—they have to have the computer to tell them how much to return."

"I been doing this for more'n forty years," he replied.

She nodded, "Thanks for the water. You have yourself a cool day, now."

She stepped onto the small porch and as she walked down the four steps, she looked over at the men. The three men from the Ford Ranger were standing by the Chevy pickup talking to those two men. Each had a beer in one hand and a cigarette in the other. The smoke drifted toward her and stung her nose. She wiggled her nose and lips to lessen the smokey stench.

"You men ought to help the old fellow out. Let him come sit in the shade and you tend to the store for him. He's getting on in years and you are just boys still."

One of the men straightened up, glowered, and started toward her. Another grabbed his arm and muttered something she couldn't hear. The man leaned back on the truck, but continued to watch her.

"Bye, now," she said and waved as she reached her own truck.

Inside, she poured a little water into her palm and the puppy lapped it up. She continued to offer him palms full until he had drunk half the bottle.

She cranked up, threw her arm out and yelled, "Good bye. Stay cool."

None responded. "Bunch of rude boys," she muttered. "They could at least be polite."

As she pulled back onto the road, she noticed the same pickup pull out behind her.

She crossed the one-lane bridge over Otter Creek, the truck still behind her. But at the next driveway, it pulled in, turned around, and headed back.

"Strange," she thought.

As soon as she was home, she called Salt to brag on what a wonderful puppy she had found.

"Where did you find it?' Salt asked.

"A lady over across Otter Creek had an ad in the paper."

"Otter Creek? You went across Otter Creek?"

"Sure. Why not?"

"My God, Beets. You're not even a little bit white, girl. You were in KKK country. Tell me you didn't stop at that store. It's run by the Grand Master of the state's KKK. You're lucky you got home alive."

GRANDMOTHER'S DRESSER

Malcolm was supposed to meet the contractor at seven Monday morning. He had been up most of night toting boxes from the house to his Escalade and moving them into storage. He was worn out and dragged back to his grandmother's now uninhabited house when all he wanted to do was go home and sack out.

But the contractor wanted to start early. Malcolm walked through the house with Johnnie and explained to the contractor exactly what he wanted done with the furniture before destruction-for-renovation began. "I don't want to try to hold a yard sale with a bunch of cruddy items," he said.

He pointed out which pieces of furniture to sit at the curb and which items and boxes to put on the moving truck.

"I haven't slept in two days," he said as they returned to the front door. "I'm going to walk over to Starbucks for coffee and will be back in a half-hour. I got to get some coffee. You understand what I want with all the furniture?"

Johnnie assured him he understood. Malcolm left. At Starbucks, he ordered his coffee and selected a pastry, then took a soft faux-leather stuffed chair in the corner. Two hours later, he woke up to cold coffee and an untouched pastry. He shook his head, stood up, grabbed the pastry to go, and hurried back to granny's house.

The moving truck was gone to the storage facility. Several pieces of ramshackle furniture sat at the curb. He nodded. Johnnie had understood, except the dresser that had belonged to his grandmother sat on the curb in the midst of the jumble.

Its patina absorbed sunlight but did not reflect glare. Malcolm hurried inside to get the contractor to bring the dresser back inside before the threatening rain reached them. Rain would ruin the magnificent item.

The contractor was nowhere to be found. One of his men, dusty from tearing out a plaster wall, said, "Johnnie done gone to the Home Depot for some stuff."

"Well, I need you to move that dresser off the side of the street and bring it back to the store room. It's one I am keeping. He misunderstood. It should have gone on the moving van."

"He said to take out the old dresser. That's what we did."

"You dumped out the finest piece of furniture in the house."

"It's old, like he said."

Malcolm smiled. "Yes, it's old. About three hundred years old. Hand made in the 1700s. Come on. I can carry one end and you the other. It's got to get inside before the rain comes."

"Okay," the worker said. As they walked toward the door, the man brushed dust from his denims and slapped his hands together. "Don't want to get crud on your nice piece of furniture," he said and grinned.

Malcolm muttered, "Thanks."

They stepped out onto the front porch. Malcolm gawked.

The dresser sat in the bed of a pickup that had already begun to move away. Its battered, rusty body told him he was seeing a junk man's truck. But a junk man with knowledge of furniture. He had left the 1950s flimsy items behind. Malcolm yelled, but the truck continued down the street.

Malcolm ran for his Escalade, turned around in the driveway and pursued. Four blocks later, a traffic light stopped the truck. Malcolm jumped out, ran to the door, and confronted the driver.

An old man, probably in his eighties, looked back.

"What's got a burr under your saddle?" he said. "You been chasing me."

"You got my dresser," Malcolm said. "It wasn't supposed to go. It was my grandmother's. It's valuable. I want it back."

"Well, you put it out on the street. You put it out, it's anybody's to pick up. And I got it and *finders-keepers*. It's mine and I'm goner keep it."

"You can't just go to somebody's yard and take things."

"It weren't exactly in your yard. It was on the street. Out there with all that other junk."

"It was not on the street. It was in the yard."

"Mister, don't you know that the first feet of your yard don't belong to you? They's part of the street. You just get to keep the grass cut. It was on the street part of your yard. It's mine now."

"Well, if it was on the street's part of the yard, it doesn't belong to you. It belongs to the city. So you stole from the city. I got your tag number and I've got a cell phone and I'm calling the police."

"You go on and do that. I'm going to city hall and take them this here dresser to use in they office for storing stuff." The light changed and the old man drove off.

Malcolm hurried back to his car, but the Mustang behind him honked and moved around. It was followed by three other cars. The light changed and Malcolm slapped the steering wheel. He didn't dare try a left turn against a red light onto a major busy street.

He cursed the traffic engineers at every light that caught him. As he neared city hall, here came the Norfolk-Southern with its hundred-plus flat cars loaded with containers from China. It took fifteen minutes to crawl through the intersection.

The truck with the dresser was parked behind city hall, near the back door. The old man stood beside the truck and talked to a gent in a suit. Malcolm pulled up, parked slantwise in front of the truck and scrambled out.

"Hey," he shouted. "That's my dresser. The old man stole it from my yard."

The suit looked at Malcolm and back to the old man. "That so? You got it from his yard?"

"No. Like I told him, once it goes onto the part of the yard that belongs to the street, it don't belong to him no more. I make my living, such as it is, from stuff folks got no use for anymore. He told me it belonged to the city since it was on the city land, so I brung it here to the city for you folks to use fer storing stuff. I thought it might go to the dump elseways. I'm sure the mayor will spin off the fifty dollars to have this here chester drawers in his office."

The suit pulled out his wallet, removed a fifty-dollar bill, handed it to the old man, and said, "I'll take one end and you the other. We wouldn't want to mess up this beautiful piece of furniture this gentleman donated to the city."

He turned back to Malcolm. "If you'd like, we can put a plaque on the side to indicate you donated it."

"You just hold up there," Malcolm said and stepped in front of the door. "I'm calling my lawyer."

He speed-dialed the attorney on his cell phone and said, "Ziggy, I need you here. Now."

"Where? Oh. I'm at the back door of city hall. Some junk dealer got my granny's dresser, you know the one, the one my great-great something dad bought from some Quaker's family back about three hundred years ago. Now he's trying to give it to the city." Pause. "Okay, Ziggy, just get here quick as you can."

Meanwhile, the suit had chatted on his cell. The two folded their phones almost simultaneously. The suit said, "Duncan is on his way down."

"Duncan? What's the stupid DA got to do with this?"

"Well, he can determine the law on the matter."

"Ziggy will determine the law on the matter."

Malcolm crossed his arms and stood sentinel at the door.

Both attorneys arrived and hovered with their callers. Ziggy said, "Malcolm, Duncan knows to the penny how much you donated to his opponent last year. He's going to determine that the dresser belongs to the city."

"He can't. He just can't."

"Technically, when you put something out on the street for the trash man to pick up, it's anybody's game. It belongs to the city, but if someone else picks it up, well, the city is not going to protest. And that joker wants to give it back to the city just to keep you from having it. Not much I can do except demand the city put it up for auction. That'll appease Duncan. He can get back at you by getting in your pocket. He doesn't give a hoot about the dresser, knowing him."

The two lawyers huddled and agreed to an auction. The city would have to advertise in the legal section of the weekly paper, so it would be three weeks before the auction. Meanwhile, the dresser would remain in city hall, in the small rotunda where it could be seen by anyone interested in bidding.

Three weeks later, only four bidders showed up, Malcolm, two local men, and a stranger. Malcolm opened with a bid of $100.00. The stranger countered with $30,000.

Malcolm turned to the stranger. "You got to be kidding. That's just my granny's dresser. I want to buy it back. It's not a thirty-thousand-dollar piece of furniture."

The stranger said, "I'll match any bid you make. Five hundred thousand? A million? That's not just a piece of sentimental furniture. It's rare. Want to keep on bidding? My museum will go up to five million."

THE PHONE CALL

When the phone rang, she answered. She never failed to answer, even at 3:30 in the night. Of all people, it was the last person she expected to hear from, the man she thought, she hoped, was gone from her life.

"Hi. You doing okay?"

"What do you want? It's the middle of the night."

"Now, what makes you think I want something?"

"Five years after the divorce and you call? What do you want?"

"I need some money. A thousand or else."

"I don't have any. You managed to use up what I had. Good bye and don't call again."

"Whoa. I know you have money. That old grandpa finally died and left you plenty. I saw it in the paper."

"Frank, I'm going to hang up. Like I said, don't call again."

"Then you'll have to bury me."

"Not likely—"

The gunshot sound blasted into her ear and seemed to explode through her head. *Gunshot. The stupid bastard has finally shot himself.*

She laid the receiver on the bedside table. He didn't know she had a cell phone. She walked into the kitchen where it was on the charger, lifted it and called 911.

"911. What is your emergency?"

"I think my ex has shot himself."

"What? Where is he? Is he with you?"

"No, he's on the other end of a phone call. He called me on my land line. Can't the police trace where he called from? I don't have caller ID on the land line."

"Yes. Hold on and I'll give you the police."

When the desk sergeant answered, she told him what happened. He transferred her again, this time to a detective. She went through the events again.

"Don't hang up your land line," he said after he took that number.

"Please call me back on my cell when you know something," she said. "Meanwhile, I'm going back to bed."

She carried the cell phone with her and laid it on the pillow next to her head. She couldn't sleep. Her mind walked back through so many events. In their third year of marriage, trouble began. She discovered he gambled. Not just on a Braves ball game once in a while, but constantly. On the lottery, where at least he had won a couple of times. But those two times only fueled his need to risk more.

Twice he had threatened to kill himself if she didn't help him out of trouble. Promised he would quit gambling. She discovered he had emptied their joint account and she had struggled to keep bills paid on her small salary. When he threatened her with suicide the first time, she had been afraid he would kill her first. She had re-financed the house— it was in her name only—but the second time, he had backed her into a corner with his demands. Loomed over her as if he would harm her. His pistol lay on the dresser to her right, in easy reach of either of them. She ducked under his arm and ran from the room. He had followed her and said, "I'm going for a walk," and gone out the front door.

She had fled back home to her parents, had her mail re-directed to her childhood address, and sought a divorce. Along with it came a restraining order for him to never be in touch or within one hundred yards of her again.

Five years ago. And now he was back. This time, the threat seemed to be real if he did in fact shoot himself. If he didn't, maybe the cops would take action and send him to a rehab center or to a psycho center for life.

Her cell phone jingled "Rudolph," and she flipped it open.

"This is Detective Ernest. We talked a few minutes ago. We are at the address he called from, but he isn't here. No one is."

"He's crazy. I afraid he's on his way here. To kill me."

"Lock your doors. I'll have a car on the way and I'll be there too as soon as I can."

Although she knew the doors were locked and the alarm was set, she checked both. She went to the closet where she kept firearms. The revolver was familiar—she had owned it since she was in her teens and a detective friend, now long dead, had taught her to shoot. But the shotgun, heavier and more awkward to handle, was deadlier.

She chose the .12-gauge single shot. If he came after her with a gun, she would have only one shot anyhow, and this one was lightweight. She went back to the bedroom, but not to bed.

The window overlooked her driveway and the street. She watched for the police cars. Time seemed to drag slower than Leap Year.

They ought to be here by now.

Someone rang the doorbell. *It can't be the police. Their cars haven't gotten here. It must be him. No way I'm going to answer it.*

But she got up and slipped down the hallway to the living room door. The world was quiet. Then the bell rang again, steadily. He was there.

"Come on, cops. Where are you?"

Small noises at the front door. Metallic. *He's got lock picks. He's going to get in.* She eased across the living room, away from the hall leading to the bedroom, and sneaked behind the kitchen door.

The front door opened.

The silhouette outlined against the street light held a pistol to his side, in his right hand. It pointed down.

He stepped inside.

Distant sirens grew louder.

"So you called the cops?" he muttered.

He hasn't seen me. I'll not move.

He turned toward the hallway. She stood in the shadows behind the kitchen door.

Flashing lights turned her front doorway alternately red and blue.

Her ex scurried out of sight.

Two policemen came to the door, pistols in hand, but instead of entering, they flanked the doorway.

"Ma'am? Are you okay? Is he in the house?"

She called. "Yes, he's inside. Down the hallway to your right as you enter. I'm safe. In the kitchen."

Two officers came in and turned down the hallway, pistols extended. They disappeared down the hall.

Three shots.

Silence.

Her insides cramped and she felt her heart slamming against her ribs. Oh *my gawd, he shot the policemen.*

A figure appeared at the end of the hall. She raised the shotgun. Held it steady and waited. She wasn't about to shoot one of the officers.

It wasn't a uniform. No holster on the waist, no Billy club. Jeans and his always light-tan shirt. The police flashers turned his face red and blue.

He raised the pistol and started toward the kitchen, toward her.

She raised her shotgun.

"Leave, or I'll shoot."

"Yeah, you ain't got the guts."

She slipped behind the door jamb, reached for the pan on the end of the kitchen counter, and threw it toward him.

He shot at the noise. Twice.

She pulled back the hammer on the single shot, threw it to her shoulder.

A shot came from the hallway and her ex fell. One of the officers staggered from the hallway into the living room.

She pointed the shotgun to the ceiling, released the hammer, and leaned the weapon into the corner.

A voice called, "Ma'am, please call an ambulance. My partner's hurt worse than me." The cop collapsed in the doorway.

HOW TO (NOT) DEER HUNT

Dick had never hunted deer. Actually, he had never been in the woods except to hike in a national park here and yonder. From his hike in Yellowstone, where the elk just watched him and the buffalo paid him no heed, he decided hunting deer didn't take much effort or specialized knowledge. Just tote your rifle into the woods and take your pick.

Everyone in the office talked deer hunting, even the women. But only to each other—not to him. After all, he was their new boss and a Yankee to boot, so they kept their distance. When the conversations he overheard indicated his employees excelled in the sport he had to be careful to only nod and not speak. He remembered his mother's caution from forty years ago—*It is better to remain silent and be thought a fool than to speak and remove all doubt.* So he remained silent, listened and did not reveal his ignorance about hunting.

When Christmas came along and the conversations turned to turkey hunting, he decided he had to do something or forever be an outcast in the company division he supervised. He got an issue of the statewide hunting publication they often discussed and looked through the ads. No luck. It was mid-June when he found a tract of land available for hunting lease and immediately signed a five-year contract for deer and turkey hunting.

He hied himself to the Wynn Brothers' Gun Shop up near Atlanta, an almost two-hour drive from Tickleboro. At least if any of his employees ventured to a gun shop, they'd go to Bass Pro in Macon.

He gathered information from the firearms expert and invested in an H&K 308. The telescopic sight set him back almost as much. At the salesman's recommendation, he added a shoulder strap and an extra clip.

Admitting he had not shot a firearm before, he asked for instructions and spent more than an hour at their gun range, with an instructor helping him sight in the rifle and learn how to hold steady by wrapping the strap around his elbow. At the end of the hour, he was plunking holes in the bullseye and was assured he would be able to kill a deer.

"You need a box of cartridges and license," the salesman said. "And where are you going to hunt? You have to have permission. From your accent, you're from up North. You got a place here to hunt?"

"Oh, I have a contract. I rented a tract of land. I'll be the only one there."

Fortunately, the store could sell the license. And a camouflage outfit that looked a little bit like the woods. He bought the twenty-cartridge box and as he walked out the door, was called back. He needed a blaze-orange vest.

When he left, he was ready to hunt. Now all he needed was the arrival of opening day in October.

At least he thought he was ready.

Opening day of hunting season arrived and off into the woods he wandered. And wandered. Not a deer poked his nose into the opening in front of him. He walked about a hundred miles over the 900 acres he paid ten thousand dollars for exclusive hunting rights. What a waste, he thought when the season ended.

Dick traveled back to the Wynn Brothers' Gun Shop and asked Jerry the salesman how come he never saw a deer. "I must have walked a hundred miles," he said.

"You aren't going to walk up on a deer. You have to wait for it to walk up to you until you learn how to sneak around in the woods. That takes years to learn. Even then, chances are slim you'll get a deer. What about your food plots? What did you plant?"

"Food plots? What are they?"

So Jerry explained, "Food plots will lure in the deer. And you need a hidey-hole, called a deer stand, to overlook the food plot. And look over the land in February for shed antlers. Then you'll know where the bucks are moving. Put your food plots in the nearby fields."

Jerry advised him on what to plant and where to buy seeds and to find a local farmer who would do the planting.

Every weekend in February and March, he walked his lease. Old cattle paths had become deer trails. On an oak hillside he found two shed antlers. Less than a hundred yards away was an abandoned hayfield, perfect for the food lot Jerry had told him to arrange.

Dick had seven food plots and a tower hidey-hole overlooking each one. He invested in a grunt call and drove his wife nuts when he walked around trying to grunt like a buck. She threatened to divorce him if he continued to carry on at home.

Opening day, long before sunrise, he stomped his way across two-thirds of the land, to the largest—and farthest—food plot, dragged himself, his rifle and bag of equipment up into his tower, and grunted.

Four hours later, he had not seen a deer and his bladder yelled at him. He relieved himself through the window of the stand, gathered up his gear and went home.

Dick drove back to the Wynn Brothers' store to talk to Jerry again. "I don't like to keep on bothering you," he apologized. He thought he detected a bit of annoyance in Jerry's face—he seemed to be watching other customers who were studying the rack of rifles behind the counter. "But there's got to be some secret to this that no one is telling me."

He did not tell Jerry about urinating from the stand. After all, who talks about doing such?

Jerry asked him about wind direction. "And did you have any cover scent? You know the deer can smell you a mile away if they're downwind. They got a nose about as good as a bloodhound."

Jerry showed him a variety, and he decided maybe the doe-in-heat would be his best bet. The salesman assured him his choice was good. Dick paid and hurried out of the store as Jerry went to the gun counter.

That weekend, Dick stood beside his car on the drive near the middle of his lease, wet a finger and held it up to catch the breeze. "Ah, coming from my left. I'll go that way to the corn patch."

Daylight found him only half-way to this corn patch. The night wind had dried out the leaves, and he sounded like a troop of retreating infantry as he tried to shortcut across the hardwoods to the field.

He saw deer—four different times, but his view was of white tails waving goodbye. At his stand, he decided to relieve his bladder before he went up the steps. Lot easier than aiming out the window. Not a deer entered the corn patch.

He pondered what he was doing wrong. Cover scent and wind direction in his favor. Grunt call every couple of minutes. Peek out the windows to keep a constant watch over every direction.

There just had to be more secrets to this deer hunting thing. He so wanted to kill a monster buck so he could brag. Seemed the only thing the men in the office wanted to talk about was hunting, either deer or turkey, or some exotic something out west. All he could contribute was the squirrels he had to run out of his stand one afternoon. And he wasn't about to offer such drivel into the conversation. He continued to just listen.

He hated the idea of asking for advice from the men he supervised. And he didn't want to go back to talk to Jerry again. Jerry wasn't telling him all of the secrets and had been obviously annoyed at his last visit. He decided to go to Macon to the Bass Pro Shop—no one there knew him anyhow. And maybe somebody knew something Jerry hadn't told him about.

The new salesman asked him if he had any shed antlers. "They are good to smash together like two bucks fighting. It'll pull in any buck that's not running with a doe."

"Oh, I found some last summer," he said. "They're big ones. You mean if I bang them together, the sound will pull in a buck?"

Assured it would work, he was warned to tie them together with a red surveyor's tape dangling to show he was people and not a deer in the woods.

"You don't want to get yourself shot for a buck," the salesman said.

"Nobody else hunts there," Dick said.

"Maybe not, but sometimes folks just don't stay on the right side of a lease line. You be careful out there. Especially since you're alone. Something happens, you might lie there for weeks before somebody found you."

The next morning, he washed down four donuts with three cups of coffee for breakfast, so once again he had to relive his bladder before he climbed the ladder to his stand.

Rifle over one shoulder, pack dangling over the other, and antlers hanging in front of his chest from around his neck, he began to climb. The antlers clanged on the ladder. He was twelve feet up the ladder when he saw the buck trot toward him.

Dick began to tremble. The deer stopped head up, and stared at Dick. Dick stared back. The buck's antlers extended tall and spread far outside his ears. The beams looked like baseball bats. Dick thought only of pictures he could share with his employees.

He wrapped his arm around the upright of the ladder and tugged the rifle free, laid the forward stock on the step and pointed it toward the deer. The safety was already off—he always clicked it off when he left his vehicle so he wouldn't forget when he reached his stand. He tried to pull the stock to his shoulder, began to lose his balance and his grip on the ladder. He pulled the trigger.

He tried to re-grip the ladder, missed, jerked the trigger again and began to fall. He did not see his trophy of a lifetime drop dead. He landed flat on his belly, with his rattling antlers through this torso and one tine into his heart.

Second Place, Short Fiction, Southeastern Writers Conference, 2019

WILSON BLACK AND THE TURKEY

Wilson Black, his face red with suppressed anger, walked from his doctor's office to the park and sank onto a bench. He stared unseeing at the pond where children threw bread crumbs to a flock of ducks and the water reflected ruffled images of still-winter-bare pecan limbs against a cerulean sky. His mind was back at the doctor's office. "You have to have this operation or you could have a fatal heart attack any time," the doctor had said and tried to sign him into Emory Hospital right then.

But Wilson had refused. "Next week. I'm going turkey hunting this weekend. It's the first weekend and I haven't gotten a bird in two years. I'll see you on Monday," and he had walked out.

No way I'm gonna miss the entire the season. Besides, it's finally warming up. Not going below fifty tonight and gonna hit seventy by Saturday. The birds will be back to courting like they were in that warm spell back in February. I don't dare tell Betty till I come home Sunday evening about what the doctor said. No, I think I'll skip work Monday and make it a three-day weekend. Skip tomorrow too, and go to camp this afternoon. Check out where those birds are roosting this evening and tomorrow.

He slapped both palms down on his thighs, nodded, and stood up.

He reached camp before dark, unloaded his gear, and slipped into his camouflage overalls and headed out to the area where he had heard gobblers hit the pine limbs a couple of weeks ago.

He picked up his .12 gauge and shoved two shells into the magazine and then cranked one into the chamber. And if one strolled by, it would be a dead turkey, a couple of days early, but who was to know? No one would be here till tomorrow night and if he were lucky tonight, he'd just dress it out, package it in sections, put it in the freezer and mark the date last year in case anyone looked in the freezer tomorrow night. Might be his only chance after what the doctor had said.

He unlocked the gate behind the cabin and drove his Chevy pickup through. He didn't bother to lock the gate, drove about a mile down the Jeep road and took the first left-hand turn off to the entrance to his personal hunting grounds. There he parked outside the gate and slapped on his hunting cap, but pushed the face net up over the bib. He walked in, with his shotgun in hand. He left his calls in the truck—he didn't want to make a mistake and warn the birds someone was talking love words who wasn't a hen.

He followed the main access road to the first turn off, where the woodcutters had dragged logs uphill to the logging yard. It ran alongside a ditch they all called B*ig Gulley* in honor of its depth.

Wilson stopped, glanced at the gulley and recalled his venture to the bottom the first year he hunted here. *Musta been thirty years ago now. Before Dad had his heart attack and we went down there to the creek at the bottom. Where the spring runs clear. Man, that was good water. Tasted like moss. Not at all like the spring lizards and crawfish. I think if I can get a bird, I'll go down there Monday before I go home. Get another drink.* He chuckled. *If I can scramble down that bank again, down where it's not more'n thirty feet.*

A hen clucked nearby. He forgot the ditch and listened. Leaves warned him something was approaching. From behind him and slightly to his right, moving downhill. He eased his left hand up, pulled the face mask down from the cap bib, and listened.

More feet agitated the leaves. Hens chatted as they moved toward their roost. Farther downhill, wings flapped. A gobbler called. Bird feet clawed pine limbs. The hen near him moved away to join the others.

Wilson remained a statue as twilight fell and darkened. The birds quieted, slept.

I'll get my bird in the morning. The heck with the law. Ranger Dixon won't be around, and anyhow if he shows up, I'll tell hm about my heart problem, and he'll give me a pass. I hope.

Wilson put thoughts of the ranger behind himself and went back to camp. He wrapped a potato in foil, started up his grill, laid the potato on the rack, and waited for it to bake. Meanwhile, he salted and peppered a sixteen-ounce ribeye. When he thought the potato was about baked, he grilled the steak.

Supper over, he set his alarm, stretched out on his bunk and slept.

He pushed off the alarm at 4:30 and rolled out of bed onto the cool floor of the camp house.

Floor's not freezing cold today. Weatherman must have been right when he said it'd be in the upper fifties today. Clad only in his tighty-whities, he strode to the door and pushed it open.

Moonlight flooded the field in front of him. Dew glistened in the moonlight. He grinned. *Gonna be a good day to turkey hunt.* He shivered. Time to get dressed and eat. He wore his jeans and Mossy Oak camouflage jacket and headed to town.

An hour and a half later, he had finished breakfast at the local Waffle House, returned to camp and dressed in his hunting outfit. He drove his Chevy pickup though the green gate, locked it, and took the Jeep road off to the left, toward the one-hundred acres where he alone had hunting rights. If any of the crowd came down early, they'd muddle around on the thousand acres the club hunted, and not disturb his special section.

Like it or not, he would have to be back at Emory for pre-op workup, so it was get a bird this weekend or not get one at all.

He parked at the locked the gate and set out on foot. He'd drop off the hill to his right, down the logging road toward the duck pond. Last spring, before the loggers came in, the birds had roosted on that hillside. Maybe they would be back. At least the loggers had not clear cut that area. "Thank goodness this landowner selectively cuts," he mumbled.

He removed his Remington .12 gauge and three shells from the truck cab. He loaded two shells into the magazine, cranked one into the chamber, and pushed the third one into the magazine. He pushed the safety on and reached into the bed for the hard-body hen decoy.

He headed toward Big Gulley, where he heard the birds roost last night.

Wilson wanted to sit by the oak where he'd collected a tom two years before. It was much wider at the base than his bulky, overweight body and his leafy oak camo would blend in with the tree. He found it, stuck his decoy in the ground in the trail, about fifteen yards downhill from the oak. He returned to the oak, kicked out a small hollow for his butt, and sat. He wiggled his bottom a little to be sure there were no rocks or roots under him to cause him movement later. Moonlight trickled through the overstory enough for him to see the trail off to his left. The understory, still barren from the long cold days, gave him a view out to more than 100 yards through the woods and down the trail.

"Gotta be careful about moving. They can see twice as far as I can."

He slipped his cedar box call, his face mask and gloves from his jacket pocket. He removed the camo handkerchief from between the box and the lid and lay it with care beside his right hip. He donned the mask and gloves and set his mind to wait.

Waiting in the woods for Wilson had always been pleasant, whether or not he took home a trophy or if game didn't even show up. something would highlight every day for him.

He thought back to the day he hunted beside another oak and a black rat snake had rustled the leaves behind him. He had finally analyzed the noises and expected to see a snake before it slithered into sight. Another morning, a mole had pushed up soil in front of his boots and poked its nose up, looked around, and when it spotted the human, had ducked back underground.

He had never had a squirrel sit on his boot as one friend had, but he had enjoyed a fox bringing a field mouse by, probably on her way to feed her kits. She had smelled him as she passed by, moving downwind, and then had darted away.

A jay squawked. Birds began to awaken. A crow flapped overhead and cawed.

A tom gobbled at the crow. Wilson thought he felt the earth shudder. Another answered from a tree beyond the first one. The crow hollered back.

Four toms replied to the crow.

Two weeks ago when I was trying to hear them fly up to roost, not a gobble and last night and today they're yelling their heads off. Must be the warm spell.

He eased his right hand down, lifted the box call.

Another tom gobbled, closer. He laid the call on the bulk of his belly.

I move, they gonna see me. I won't get a chance to call.

A bird yelped. Raucous. *Maybe a jake.*

Birds dropped to the ground like a bushel of apples being dumped. Four toms strutted, all too far way for a shot. Wilson did not dare move. One hen led the search for food, scratched once with one foot, twice with the other, and studied the ground to see what she uncovered. The hens ignored the toms.

Wilson eased his hands around the box call, lifted the lid to prevent any unwanted squawking, and cut his eyes down to see his hands. He slid the lid against the edge of the box in imitation of a hen's soft *I-am-ready* yelp.

The four toms gobbled and looked his direction.

They spotted not him but the decoy posed as if ready to drop to the ground to mate. The toms danced toward her.

"Come on, come on boys. Whoever gets here first gets the prize. One load of Number 2 steel and a visit to my stove."

The toms obliged. One took the lead and moved steadily forward. The others followed a few feet behind.

With their attention full on the decoy, Wilson merged his shoulder with the shotgun slower than the shadows moved across the morning. None of the toms noticed. The hens were busy searching for bugs and any acorns left from last fall.

The lead tom reached the decoy, and Wilson shot.

Birds flew and yelped fear. The tom rolled. Wilson dropped the shotgun, scrambled up and dashed toward his bird.

First lesson he learned when he started hunting, stomp your foot on the turkey's head so he can't get up and fly off, if he's not dead.

Wilson, however, did not quite reach the turkey before it rolled onto its feet and spread his wings for takeoff. Wilson lunged, his arms outstretched, hands grabbing. He caught a double-hand-full of tail feathers.

The tom flapped his wings. The tail feathers came out in Wilson's hands.

Wilson lunged again, wrapped his arms around the bird, and the two of them rolled across the trail and down the drop-off into Big Gulley.

Wilson landed head first on top of the gobbler. He would not make his medical appointment at Emory and not live to die of the predicted heart attack. His neck, like that of the bird, was broken.

THE FISHING BOY

Everybody called him simply *Boy*. He was not only the youngest, but also the only male child in a family of seven children. Pa took him everywhere—fishing down to the river when he still wore diapers, onto the oak ridges to hunt squirrels when he was six and could manage a .22 rifle, into the swamps to shoot wild hogs when he was eight and heavy enough that a 7-mm bolt action war surplus rifle's kick did not set him down.

Pa taught him that women and girls tended to the house. As men, they owned the outdoors, even if it meant milking the tan-colored Jersey and slopping and butchering the hogs. Pa taught him that anything beat working for wages or cleaning house or toting in water from the well to wash clothes.

Boy loved fishing best and begged for his own rod and reel when he saw one of the local white men with one down at the river. But Pa told him such was too expensive and would cost far more than the $25.00 he spent on the old scratched-up rifle. Maybe when he got a lot older, he could work and earn money. Pa said if he bought Boy a rod and reel, he'd have to buy all six of the girls something special too— like a new dress and shoes.

"Just keep on using that limb we cut off the hickory, or tie the line to your toe if you don't want to hold the pole all the time."

Now eighty-four, Boy moved slower and had burned to a reddish-brown except for the white forehead protected by his straw hat. He still fished as Pa taught him: A stick for the float unless he could find a real cork from a wine bottle the local drunk threw in the trash, a long line with a steel hook so the fish couldn't bend it when you caught a whopper (he never had caught a whopper), and a fifteen-foot, 50-pound line. Tie one end of the line to the big toe and throw the baited hook and stick into the river. Let the current carry it to wherever the fish were. And nap while you wait.

His bait today was red wigglers he had dug up from under a board behind Jenkins Hardware, his hook a new one Mr. Jenkins had donated mid-afternoon, after Boy caught a small sunfish and lost his worms.

Boy had used the small fish as bait. He stretched himself out in the shade of the catalpa tree that hung over the riverbank, put his straw hat over his eyes and his hands under his neck, and dozed. Jenkins shook his head and returned to the store. He figured he'd wake Boy at dark.

The sun moved shadows across Boy as the day wore on. Heat shimmered over the river. Dragonflies flittered in the weeds and rode the stems as the wind swayed the brush. When the shadows left him in sunlight and heat, he woke, moved a few yards downstream, and settled back down. He was dead asleep a half-hour later when something grabbed his bait and pulled the line tight around his toe.

The forty-pound catfish rode the current downstream and increased his own speed. The line held when it tightened and the hook set. The fish didn't slow down but pulled the line with the force of an angry mule.

The sudden jerk woke Boy as he slid down the bank and into the river, right foot first. His left leg buckled under him. He screamed and went under.

But he was alone at the river.

The fish pulled Boy into the deeper, swifter current and to the bottom while Boy swung his arms in a failed attempt to reach the surface. He couldn't swim.

When Jenkins returned to see what Boy had caught, he thought the old man had gone home. "Whatever happened to Boy?" became the topic of conversation at dinner tables and the local pub in Tickleboro for years.

THE REKINDLED LOVE AFFAIR

She didn't want to go to the party. Just one more informal cocktail party for the host and hostess to get into bank accounts for some political candidate running for who knows what office. Half the folks would be tipsy from the constant supply of full champagne flutes passed through the ballroom. What better way to entice people to open up their checkbooks.

She sighed. She had to go. Ten years ago, when, unmarried and not out of college, she gave birth to her son, no one considered inviting her to any event. But once grandpa died and she inherited his fortune, she became the prize catch for every social event in town. Money, always money, she thought.

Well, at least it wasn't formal. She could get by with an informal dress or even a pants suit. She would leave early, with a promise to send a check. That way, her chauffeur could drive her and there would be no need to carry a purse—or her checkbook.

And she could arrive a bit late and leave a bit early.

She strode into a crowded room and was greeted by a tuxedoed waiter carrying a tray of champagne flutes. She accepted one and looked over the crowd. Mayor and his cronies. Two of the three county commissioners. Even the sheriff. All up for reelection in three weeks.

Her gaze locked onto a tall black-haired man talking to the local priest. *Is that really Calvin? I don't believe it. It's been ten years and not a word from him since college. Since he left me pregnant and vanished from my life. I wonder if he ever married. If so, does she know he has a son? No, I doubt if he knows himself. I sure thought I was in love with him.*

She watched him chatting with the priest and two other men, men who, she knew, were big political contributors. More so than she was. They had big businesses to run—all she had was the trust fund. Although the fund topped a hundred million, she received only a couple of million from it annually. Her job at the newspaper kept her in pocket change, kept her off the streets, out of trouble and in a position to reveal everyone else's troubles.

She hadn't been in trouble but once. That was the term she used when she told her parents. "Mama, I'm in trouble."

Calvin had been graduated for two days and gone to England for postgraduate work at Cambridge as a Rhodes Scholar when her period was late and she realized she was pregnant.

But he was gone. He had promised to write, to send her his address, but he never did. She faced the nine months with her angry parents, but when the boy was born, they fell in love with their grandchild.

She drifted around the room. When she stopped to chat with a group, she stood so she could watch him. Half an hour she watched. He had not seen her.

Her host took her by the arm and said, "There's someone here I want you to meet." He led her toward Calvin.

He looked up as they approached. Joy flooded his face and he stepped away from the group he was chatting with.

"Katrina! How wonderful to see you again."

"You know each other?" the host asked.

"Yes, we went to college together," Calvin answered. "It's been a long time,"

"About ten years," Katrina replied. She wanted to take him into another room and begin their affair again. Or maybe just kill him.

His eyes softened as they had when they were about to make love. She returned the expression, but his face hardened quickly as if he feared someone would recognize they had once been lovers.

She heeded and returned the indifferent look, as they had so often in college to hide their affair.

"I am glad to see you again, Cal. But I have to leave. If you'll give me a call—I'm in the book—maybe we can get together for lunch and relive old times."

"It would be my pleasure, Katrina. I'm in town for a couple of weeks before I have a trip to Italy. I'll call tomorrow. Maybe we can lunch this week."

He didn't wait until tomorrow. He called a little after ten that night and his first words were, "May I come over?"

"Yes. Don't forget. Play it safe. Bring condoms." *No way I'm telling him about Sam. At least he's at summer camp. I'll kept his room closed off.*

He brought condoms, and they began another affair, but limited to ten-midnight every night.

For the four days, their conversations had been recollections and "do you remember...?"

"I leave for Italy in two more days," he told her. "I will miss you like crazy."

"Italy would be a wonderful place for a honeymoon. We used to talk about going together, to explore Rome especially."

"Oh, darling, I love you, but I can't marry. I'm a priest."

"Oh, darling, I know. Why do you think I've had that sound-activated video-recorder running every night? Now you have a choice. Resign your priesthood and we get married, or get thrown out of the church, probably be excommunicated."

"You can't be serious."

"I am deadly serious. And don't worry about getting a job. There's not much work for an ex-priest. But I have my grandfather's trust fund. I get a couple of million a year to spend. We can live on that. Of course, I've been living mostly on my salary as editor of the local paper. It's a great way to tell secrets."

He left the priesthood. The wedding date was set, invitations sent out. He stood at the altar in the crowded church. The organist began playing the processional, and everyone stood up.

The priest raised a hand. The organ quieted. He said, "I've been asked to give this envelope to Calvin before the bride comes down the aisle." He smiled. "I think it's her prepared wedding vows."

He handed a sealed envelope to Calvin who tore it open. He stared at the elaborate penmanship he remembered from college days.

"Sorry, Cal. You taught me about dependability in love. I'm gone. Probably won't see you again. Happy life."

REVENGE FOR THE DEER

She was returning from a morning's deer hunting when she saw the buzzards floating overhead, black silhouettes against the scattered clouds and winter-blue sky. *That's too many for a road-kill possum. Must be a deer or one of Jackson's cows.* The circling birds drifted northward with the thermals, passed overhead and across her pasture.

Somebody hit a deer.

She went inside, pulled off her hunting outfit, unloaded her rifle and placed everything on her bed. She returned to her Chevy truck to check out the road.

Recently paved and with a mile-long strait-away it had become an invitation for the local town boys to drag race. One of them had probably hit a deer.

Driving so slowly several cars roared by, she studied the shallow ditches. No carcass and no perched buzzards, but a lot of trash and beer cans discarded by the newly installed wannabe-country-folks in the new development, people who didn't know a turkey from a chicken.

She went home for a late breakfast. *I'll call Jackson and see if he's lost a cow and then I'm going to have a nice long nap.*

Jackson didn't answer his phone. *Must still be milking.* She left a message.

An hour into her nap, her cell phone rang. Jackson reported he had not lost any cattle and had seen the buzzards. "Enough of them to clean up a battlefield," he summed up his opinion.

"I think it's a deer, then," she said. "I'll see what I can find. I'll let you know if I find anything."

She decided to scout her front pasture—what had been the *front pasture* when her folks were alive and kept cattle in the 250 acres in front of the house and horses in the *back pasture*.

The land was patched with pine and mixed hardwoods between large meadows she kept mowed. Every early fall, she planted strips of food along the edge for the wildlife. Persimmons were still plopping down and acorns had been dropping for a more than a week. Deer, wild turkeys, and quail fed over her land as heavily as the cattle once did.

She hoped to find buck signs—fresh scrapes along the hedgerow of oaks on the ridge. Maybe a few trees with bark rubbed off, a combination that would mean Old Buster Buck was in a courting mood and pawing out his invites to the does.

She decided to take her Ruger .44 with iron sights on her stroll into the woods, just in case Old Buster Buck decided to show himself. She slung it onto her shoulder and as she stepped onto the porch, shadows drifted across her yard.

Damn. I thought maybe they drifted away, but they're back. Those buzzards have to be after something close by.

They seemed concentrated to her north, so she strode out that direction and decided rather than scouting out the woods, she would walk the edge and watch the buzzards.

Yep. They're after something on my place, not on the road.

A quarter of a mile down her wood line, she saw them. Some perched on the broken remains of limbs on a forty-foot tall pine snag. Some drifted on the thermals. As she neared, a black cloud flapped into the air.

The stench reached her and she coughed to get the odor from her mouth and nose. "As bad as one of our dead cows. And I'm upwind."

Following the edge a few yards, she turned down the Jeep trail into the woods. Three carcasses greeted her, rib cages in various degrees of eaten flesh, hides shredded and the ground black with gore.

Not much left after the coyotes, foxes and buzzards. Probably from two or three days ago. Probably Wednesday, when I heard all that shooting.

Three bucks, two of the nice eight-point yard bucks and the seven pointer I've gotten on the trail camera. At least they're not Buster.

But who in Sam Hill did this? No way anybody has been in here. No poacher would have left these. Not with those antlers. A poacher would have taken the antlers if nothing else. And howcome all three here together?

Possibilities rumbled through her mind and settled down to one.

They got shot, only injured, fled, and came here to hide. And died. Sooo, where were they...?

She turned back into the field and looked toward the road. *Charlie-boy Fowler. He hunts over corn. I found it last year when that goody-goody was in church. Only it was gone when the ranger checked it out. I'll figure out what to do.*

She crossed the field toward the dirt road and the direction of Charlie-boy's stand. The ground, still damp from the downpour

Tuesday night, was like a handbook on tracking deer: Clumps of sod showed where deer had stumbled across the meadow and torn up the ground as they fled. *All dead in one place, had to have been shot in one place. I'll do something tomorrow while Charlie-boy and family are in church.*

She pondered discussing the situation with law enforcement and knew she would not ask for help. Not even from the ranger in the next county. The local ranger had arrested Charley's uncle two years ago and been moved to another district. Any new case would get the same treatment: It would go to the local court, where Charley's father was judge. He had never recused from any case and was responsible for the ranger being transferred. What part of the county Papa didn't own, Charley himself controlled as sheriff. And if anything in surrounding counties needed to be handled, Papa's brother the state senator tended to that issue.

Tomorrow came. She prepared for her trespassing and illegal actions. She shoved her feet into the old Ted Williams kangaroo boots she had worn years ago and never could bear to discard. Although no rain was predicted, she donned a plastic camouflage rain suit and taped the legs to the top of her boots. A pair of lightweight cotton gloves covered her hands. She pulled a threadbare Braves cap snug over her head.

She loaded tools into her truck and drove to her fence line where she could watch her neighbor's driveway.

When she saw their bright red Mercedes pull out of their driveway and turn toward town, she drove back down her fence line and parked. The brush was thick here, and the deer crossed the fence elsewhere rather than try to push their way through. Careful that her rain suit not get snagged, she eased through the brush, crossed the road, and entered Jackson's land some hundred yards south of his landline with the Fowler's. She headed toward the Fowler's and trespassed without any concern of legality.

Fifty yards across onto the Fowler's land, she spooked deer. One snorted three times. She saw four white tails bouncing away.

She found the ladder leaned against a hickory. A fancy, five-hundred-dollar ladder stand, painted camouflage, topped with a wide seat, a wraparound gun rest, and a camouflage net to hide the hunter and his feet from deer approaching from any direction.

Deer tracks and droppings covered the ground only a few yards in front of the stand. She smelled the does, but the musk smell was far stronger. Corn was scattered in a crisscross pattern of lines, broken in a few places where deer had fed.

Musta been out here before going to church. He'll be back this afternoon.

Overhead, birds and squirrels let her know she was intruding on their noon meal.

"Glad I brought this," she muttered as she hefted the bolt cutters. She cut off three adjacent steps half-way up the ladder, cut them in half, left the pieces where they fell, and headed for the truck. *No way they can use that stand again unless he hauls it to a welder to put in new steps. And if Charley-boy does and sets it back up or buys another one, I'll cut off one of the legs.*

I got myself more throw-away outfits that he's got ladders. I can outlast him.

When she reached her truck, she removed hat, rain suit, boots and gloves, slipped her feet into her usual hunting boots, used a rag to wipe down the bolt cutters and threw them into the truck bed, stuffed all the DNA-bearing evidence into a garbage bag, and joined another dozen locals at the county dumpster.

THE OLD LADY AND THE WOODEN SPOOLS

When June turned eighty her two sons had celebrated with her with a night out on the town the evening before and a party at Kurtis's home the afternoon of the birthday. The last four living members of her college sorority came, but unlike her, they were doddering along with the aid of walkers.

She still walked with the same stride that carried her into the woods for years to hunt deer, into the fields for quail, and to the edge of meadow and woods for the wily and elusive wild turkey.

Her college roommate Elsie told her, "At eighty you got to downsize, get rid of things now because your children have told mine, they don't want any of your old family things. Too heavy and dark. My son Eddie told me he didn't want the old glass oil lamp my great-grandfather used when he was a student at Washington and Lee when General Lee himself was president. If they don't want something as valuable as that lamp, they don't want anything that doesn't come from Ikea."

But June was not to be pushed into emptying her house of the heirlooms that to her were priceless historical treasures. "I can't do that," she told her friend. "I can't control what they do with things when I croak, but I'm holding onto great-grand- father's Joe Brown Pike and his cap-and-ball pistol. And the cradle hand-made by my ancestor who fought in the French and Indian War. I've got everything listed, with pictures, of who owned it before it came down the line to me. If they've got any sense, they'll treasure it all."

Two days later, June went back to the northern part of the county where she had been introduced to deer hunting more than fifty years ago by a young man she thought she would marry. The young man had not become her husband, and after they broke off their romance he married a girl from out of state. June had not been back to his family's mansion or the vast plantation. He died years ago, but his widow, according to rumors, had become a recluse. Her obituary ran in the paper a few days ago, and burial was to be back in her home state. Curiosity drove June, curiosity and the new Subaru Forester she had given herself as a birthday gift to the chagrin of her sons who thought she was wasting her money.

The mansion stood shaded by massive oaks that she remembered as saplings. *Well, it has been more than fifty years.*

To her surprise, a hand-painted sign out front stated: "Estate sale. All must go." No other cars around except for a new tan Ford 150 pickup. Through the truck window she spotted a gun rack and three rifles.

Guess Tommy's nephews still hunt.

She parked in the shade of the nearest oak and strode up the path to the front porch where a man in camouflage rocked in the chair June remembered had belonged to Tommy's grandmother and used to sit before the fireplace in the living room. It did not belong on a porch where heat and moisture would separate its joints.

He shifted his wad of tobacco into the back of his jaw and said, "Morning, Ma'am. You here about the sale?"

She smiled. "Yes, I am. I knew Tommy when we were kids. About sixty years ago."

"Yes, Ma'am. Well, come on in. See what you like. It's all for sale. Let me know what you want. I ain't had time to put prices on it all yet. We gonna put an ad in the paper this Thursday." He learned forward and spat a dark stream into the yard.

She tried not to show her disgust and thanked her god that she had not married Tommy and lived with his relatives, rich though they might be. "Thank you," she said and entered the hallway. Nothing had changed since she was here. Eighteen-inch wide pine boards rose sixteen feet to the ceiling. Gold-bordered mirrors faced each other across the ten-foot-wide hall. She remembered counting herself reflected from one to the other.

She turned to the right, into what had been the parlor. It was now a sewing room. She had heard Matilda liked to make her own dresses, but apparently, she had never discarded anything.

Cardboard boxes lined two walls. June looked into a box.

"Good god almighty!" June whispered. "I can't believe it. There must be fifty years of spools here."

A glance into the next box showed more spools, and more in the next one.

"Matilda's grandmother must have saved spools too," June muttered. "Some of these go back more than a hundred years. I got to find out what he wants for them."

When she asked, he replied. "Oh, them spools ain't worth nothing. I was gonna use them for kindling if they were around when it got cold.

You want 'em, I can put 'em in the trunk of your car. Just charge you $5.00 to load 'em if that's alright."

"That will be fine," she said.

Half an hour later, she drove home with seven boxes of spools. *The boys'll dig me up and beat me to death if I die before I get all of these sold. I'll call Maggie and get her over here tomorrow. I'll bet there's several thousand dollars' worth of kindling in those boxes. They don't even make spools out of wood anymore. Just out of plastic. Some of these are for spinning wheels, too.*

At home, she hauled them into her back room and went to the telephone to call Maggie. She got the answering machine. "The shop is closed for the week. I'm taking a vacation. Call me Monday."

Monday was four days away. June left her message, "I got a thousand and one items you won't believe I'd sell. Call me when you can come give me a price and load them up!"

As she started upstairs to go to bed, her two cats ran down the steps in a screaming fight and tripped her. As she landed, she knew her hip was broken. But, thankful for the boys' insistence that she have one of those buttons for "I've fallen and I can't get up," she pulled it from inside her blouse and pushed the button.

"Are you all right, Miss June? Do you need help?"

"I'm not right at all, and I do need help. I've fallen and busted my hip and need the ambulance and need you to call my son Kurtis at home." She gave the number, and soon heard the ambulance wailing its arrival.

The doctors agreed with her diagnosis and said they would operate in the morning to pin her hip back together. Unused to pain and unused to receiving orders, she rebelled and kept herself sedated with the pain pump. Pneumonia struck and June was moved into ICU.

Two weeks later she returned to a private room for another two days before she could go home. Driving her home, Kurtis told her Maggie had been by and was happy with the deal they made. She simply nodded. All she was interested in was getting home to grandpa's bed.

Kurtis parked the car. As she hobbled toward the front door, he said, "I hope you like what I did with the money from Maggie. She sure wanted all that thousand and one things."

She opened the front door to find her treasures gone and the house completely furnished with Ikea.

JUDGE STONE AND THE MOONSHINERS

Judge Benjamin Franklin Stone was sick and tired of having to go down from Atlanta to every rinky-dink town in South and Middle Georgia to hold court for the local moonshiners. It seemed that the local juries were the bootleggers' customers and would never find the culprit guilty for fear of losing a chance at the product. No matter how strong the evidence, the jury always found some excuse to not believe the revenue agent. Never did the local sheriff bring a case. He wondered if the rumors were true, that the sheriff in some of these towns distributed moonshine himself.

He "harrumphed" aloud as he parked his two-year old 1937 Caddy Fleetwood in front of the Baptist Church. One more *holy court*. Maybe this time he would not have to spend the night in some flea-bag motel twenty miles away on the two-lane pot-holed road between here and Macon.

He entered the sanctuary door and surveyed the room. He saw the same setup he had become accustomed to. A pastor's chair for him, card tables for him and the prosecutor and defense attorney, and folding chairs for them and for whoever served on the jury.

There would be none of the usual formality. No bailiff to announce for everyone to stand. No need for his robes today, and besides he still didn't have an idea where he would don his robe or even if the chorus had a room for changing into robes. All he ever saw was the sanctuary.

It was too hot anyhow for his robes, and it wasn't like back home, where if it was too hot he could just wear his undershorts beneath the robe and no one would know the difference.

He walked down the center aisle to the front, and as he approached the card table with the attorneys sitting, they both rose. Two familiar faces.

"Morning, Your Honor," they said simultaneously.

"Morning, Mr. Bates, Mr. Lawrence."

He went to his chair, sat, then stood and removed his suit jacket and draped it over the back of the chair. Off to the side, sitting in folding chairs, were twelve men. Country men, in overalls who, he suspected, had already been chosen to serve as the jury.

"Okay, folks, ready for this trial?" he asked as he sat.

The two attorneys continued to stand. "Yes, sir," they replied in unison.

He nodded, and the lawyers sat.

"Okay, let's get this show on the road. Do we have a jury pool?"

The sheriff stepped forward and replied, "Yes, sir. These here men," He pointed to the group.

"Any objections from the prosecution or the defense?" Judge Stone asked.

Both lawyers rose. "No sir."

Judge Stone wondered if they practiced speaking together. They had echoed each other when they argued before him months ago. "Aren't either of you going to question these potential jurors? Mr. Lawrence, what about the prosecution?"

The prosecutor shrugged and shook his head.

"Mr. Bates? Is the defense content with this jury?"

"Yes, Your Honor. I am satisfied. I have no questions."

Judge Stone studied the jurors. *Yep, looks like the same bunch I've seen before. Might as well get this* not guilty *case over with and get back home. I could use a good cocktail and steak and I sure don't want either down here.*

The prosecutor called its first witness, Federal Revenue Agent Paul Madison.

At least it's a new agent, the judge thought. *Maybe they won't make a fool of him. He looks intelligent, but then I know how wily Bates can be. I've seen him make a fool out of a prosecution witness before.*

The sheriff swore Agent Madison in and Lawrence began his questions. Name, job, history of arrests and convictions.

Huh. Never lost a case. This might be a guilty verdict after all and I can send the culprit off to jail. He looks like a kid even if he has to be eighteen. Be a shame to put him in with the hardened criminals. Have to do it, however.

Prosecutor Lawrence did his job, carefully working the agent from the day he found the still, to his day-to-day observations and through the series of photographs he had taken with the defendant stirring mash, running off the whiskey and collecting it in Mason jars. The pictures went to the judge and then passed hand-to-hand from juror to juror.

Lawrence asked the agent for his sample of the whiskey he had collected before he destroyed the still. He produced a Mason jar of clear liquid.

A juror raised his hand and spoke. "Judge, I got a question."

Judge Stone looked at the juror. "Yes? What is it?"

"How can we know that-there stuff is whiskey unless we get to taste it ourselves?"

"You are supposed to take the word of this witness. He is under oath."

"Yep, we know that, Judge. But we don't know if he knows what real whiskey is."

Stone threw up his hands in surrender. "Okay, okay. Let the jury taste the contents of that jar. Sheriff, get some cups."

"Oh, Mr. Judge, we don't need no cups. We always pass the jar along in the woods when we test our likker, and we can pass it right along here."

And so they did. Eleven men each took a swallow, wiped his palm across the lip of the jar, rubbed the back of his hand over his own lips, and passed the jar along.

When it reached the twelfth man, he complained. "There ain't nothing left here for me to even get a taste. How can I vote on it being good likker if I ain't had a taste?"

Judge Stone shook his head. "You just do the best you can with the evidence presented. Mr. Lawrence, if you please, continue with your questions."

"That's all I have, Your Honor."

Defense Attorney Bates stood, hooked his thumbs into his overall straps, and asked, "Agent Madison, are you positive this defendant is the person you photographed and later arrested at the still in question?"

"My word on it. I am positive. It couldn't be anyone else. Just look at the pictures."

Attorney Bates turned to the back of the room, where a deputy sheriff stood beside the sanctuary door, and said, "Deputy, please open the door."

As it opened, two young men entered and walked down the middle aisle of the sanctuary.

"Are you sure one of these is not the man you saw at the still? Can you now swear you arrested the right man?"

"Oh, my God. Triplets."

The crowd hooted. The judge stood, called, "Case dismissed," and walked out of the church.

NEVER MISS AN OPPORTUNITY

Martha and Dave sat on the front porch of their imitation ante-bellum mansion. They had backed their chairs up to the wall to avoid the blowing rain. Anyone passing by on the river would think they were seeing a home that survived Sherman's march. On closer inspection, they might notice that it sat three feet above the ground, on stilts made of six-inch steel pipes.

Dogs could wander under without crawling. Dave's two prize bird dogs often had to chase out a wandering raccoon or possum.

The couple lived far off the highway, their dirt driveway a good mile through oak and pine woods. On evenings when they turned on the spotlights they could sit on the front porch, look toward the river and watch wildlife wander into the yard. Dave had been an avid hunter until he lost his leg in a motorcycle accident, so now he daily hobbled into the yard with a bucket of corn to scatter for whatever critters dared to venture close to the house. A pair of red foxes sometimes slipped through the shadows and snatched up kernels. For Dave, it was the two large bucks that kept his attention. The larger, a twelve point that Dave would have been so proud to have collected in his hunting days, needed to only lift his head and look toward the smaller buck for the younger one to run off.

Tonight, nothing moved except water. It had rained steadily for three days. The river was rising and water lapped over the banks.

"I think we'll be okay," Martha said. "The surveyor said with our stilts three feet up, we were higher than the 100-year flood would reach."

"I hope we don't get flooded," Dave replied. "I can't swim with this leg." He tapped his fist on the aluminum. The sound was lost in the tumult of the storm.

Martha's cell phone vibrated against her side. She reached into her jacket pocket and pulled it out. It was her son, Winston.

"Yes, Son?"

"Mom, they say the river is going to flood really high. You and Dave need to leave now. Before the water gets up to you."

"Oh, don't fret so. The river's still in its banks. But it is moving along a lot faster. It's got waves now."

Dave said, "There goes a tree."

"I heard that," Winston said. "Mom, leave now. Please."

"Oh, Winston, don't be a wuss. We're more than six feet above the river. It'll never get this high. Don't worry."

"I know the driveway is going to be a mess if it's not already. You should have fixed those potholes last fall. Take the Jeep and leave."

"No. I'm having too much fun watching the river. We're on the front porch. The wind's blowing from the other direction so we aren't even getting wet. You stop worrying. We'll call you tomorrow. Goodnight."

She disconnected.

"Winston after us to leave, is he?"

"Yeah. We're not going to have a problem. And I love the sound of the rain on the roof. I'm so glad we decided on tin for the porch roof."

They returned to silence and listened to the storm. The wind rose and limbs thudded against each other.

"I think I'll turn on the spotlights," Martha said. She stepped inside and flipped the switch. Light spread across the yard and down the slope to the river bed.

As she returned to her chair, the river roared upstream.

"That the river? It must be rising fast," Martha said.

"Maybe they opened the flood gates at the dam. If they did, we might be in trouble."

"Naw. It won't get this high."

But thirty minutes later, the water slapped against the bases of the riverside standpipes under the house.

"Let's go inside," Dave suggested. "The wind is getting colder."

When they entered the house, Martha kicked off her shoes. Dave commented, as he had for their forty-year marriage, "Barefoot girl with cheeks of tan."

She laughed, kissed his cheek and continued their family jest with, "Boyfoot bear with teaks of Chan."

They went on to the kitchen where Martha pulled the leftover stew from the fridge and poured it into a pot to warm up.

Dave pitched in fixing supper—he set the table, put ice into the tea glasses, poured the tea and sliced lemons. They sat in the dining room to eat.

Lightning and thunder exploded. "That was close," Dave said. He got up and hobbled to the front porch. The spotlights shone on the hundred-year-old white oak that had led them to pick this site for their home. It was shattered. Limbs lay every which-a-way and bare, pale, barkless wood gleamed with water in the spotlights.

Water now roiled sticks and picnic trash beneath the porch.

He returned to the kitchen. "That got the oak. It's a mess out there. And water's under the house."

"It can't reach us. Remember what the surveyor said. Take another hundred years for it to flood this high. You ready for ice cream?"

"Sure. What flavors we got?"

"Vanilla and strawberry."

"Let's do vanilla and some chocolate syrup. Any of those Girl Scout cookies left we got from Sandy?"

"I'll get them. I hid the chocolate mints from you. That's all we have left."

She returned to the table, set the ice cream bowls down and returned to the kitchen for the cookies and the chocolate syrup.

"What in the world?" Her feet were wet. "Dave, look. We *had* better leave. The water's coming up through the floor."

"We can't drive out now. Call Winston."

She dialed his cell phone and he answered on the second ring. "Yes, Mom? You and Dave ready to vacate now?"

"God, yes, Winston. Water's coming up through the floor. That surveyor promised us it wouldn't."

"Forget him, Mom. I'll be there in about ten minutes. Hank and Jesse and I are already on the river in the Riviera."

"Oh, Winston, thank you, thank you."

"Y'all stay inside. Don't even think of coming out till I get there."

She folded her cell phone and turned to Dave. "He's got the Riviera out for us. It'll handle the river like nothing."

They stood in the doorway to the porch and watched the river. Lights approached. The boat eased up toward the porch and stopped fifteen feet away. Holding onto a rope, Hank jumped over the side into waist high water. He fought to keep his balance and not yield to the thrust of the river. He pulled the rope to the stump of the oak and tied off the boat.

Winston and Jesse jumped into the water. Winston held onto a rope tied to the railing and pulled it behind him as they worked their way against the current to the porch.

He tied the end of the rope to a porch column. "Jesse, you stay here with Dave. Hank, help me tote Mom to the boat, I'll carry her and you hold onto my belt and the rope so I don't get washed down stream."

Dave sat in one of the porch chairs. "Jesse, maybe you best go to the bedroom and get my crutches. I don't need to be without them, just in case."

Jesse dashed inside. He was not back when Winston and Hank returned.

Dave stuck his head inside and yelled, "Hey, Jesse, you find my crutches?"

"Yessir," he said and ran onto the porch with the crutches.

Winston told Dave he'd carry his stepfather to the boat piggy-back. Jesse and Hank helped him get on Winston's back. The water continued to rise and was almost chest high. Jesse in front and Hank behind, the four men eased toward the boat. Winston turned his back to the boat and Dave slid over the side and onto a seat.

The three rescuers climbed aboard. Jessie and Hank released the two ropes and Winston changed the gears from *idle* to *reverse*. The current pulled at the boat. Winston pushed the gear shift forward and weaved the Riviera through the debris field back into the river bed and toward his yard.

He eased the boat across his own flooded yard until the bow struck soil. He stopped to *idle*, instructed Hank and Jesse where to find more ropes, and they secured the boat.

He dropped the ladder for his mother and helped Dave descend. As they started up the hill to Winston's house, Jesse held onto Dave to keep him from slipping. But Jesse slipped. Dave tried to hold him, but couldn't and both tumbled and rolled partway down the bank toward the river.

Winston and Hank skidded after them. Unhurt, Dave sat up and laughed as Martha slipped and slid down to him.

Jesse scrambled around on the ground, picking up something. Martha said, "Jesse, that's my jewelry you got there. You just never miss an opportunity, do you?"

He smiled. "It weren't gonna cost you nothing, Miss Martha. Don't you got insurance?"

AN OLD BOOK

Debra saw the *estate sale* sign pointing down a residential side street. She followed the arrow three blocks, turned right and drove another four blocks. She came up to a stationary traffic jam: Cars parked on both sides and only one car at a time could pass down the street. She parked her ancient Volkswagen bug behind a battered green and white Chevy pickup with enough dents to hide a bushel of apples. She got out, locked her car, and strode up the sloping road.

The house hunkered on a weedy lot like one of the Macbeth witches squatting beside her cauldron, as if it wanted to lower itself into the ground. Paint now peeled in patches on the clapboard siding, but the antebellum mansion had once ruled the block.

Columns rose from the first-floor front porch, tied into an upper porch and reached a roof trimmed with dentil work. Bees swarmed around a honey-stained hole in the upper level of the right-hand column.

The yard was cluttered. A rusted bicycle leaned against an oak whose bark had begun to grow around it. Four other bicycles leaned against the first one and each other. *Long time leaning there. It's a wonder the American Pickers haven't found this place. I think there's an old Harley over yonder, too. Well, not for me. But from the looks of the house, there's gotta be some good stuff here.*

She waved to a man sitting in the shadows of the oak trunk and figured he was waiting for his wife to buy everything she thought he could tote home. She skipped up the front steps to the house.

Inside, two ladies sat at a card table with a cash box before them. "Welcome," one said. "We have everything priced. All proceeds go to the Boys and Girls Club. The lady who died had no family. Everything is priced to sell. Take your time looking. We have items on three floors, including the basement."

"Thanks," Debra replied and began a slow walk through the crowd in the first room. Between people she spotted crystal, silverware, and *Gone With the Wind* collectibles. She smiled as she thought of the four times she had watched the movie. No, these were not for her. Too fancy to have with three young cats that liked to race each other around the house.

The next room was the library. Books. Floor to ceiling book shelves on three sides, with a sliding ladder to access the upper shelves.

The room smelled of leather and dust and reminded her of the barn where she stabled her horse.

Gotta be a few good reads here, she thought.

She eased along the right-hand wall. Biographies: Churchill. Eisenhower. Lincoln. Benjamin Harvey Hill. *Must have more than a hundred biographies.*

History. In chronological order. She moved on past Egypt, Greece and Rome to the United States.

And stopped when she spotted the dark spine and the gold design —*The Great West.*

She didn't remember an Indian being on the spine of her father's copy. *But I never really looked at the spine, I mostly curled up in the corner and read the book. And the spine on Dad's copy was torn at the bottom. Maybe the Indian was all the way torn off.*

She reached out for the book, but withdrew her hand and held it a few inches from the book for a moment. Was it the book by Henry Howe, from the 1850s, about the early, eastern-west, or one of the later books of the same name but about the west-of-the-Mississippi west?

Her brother had inherited her father's copy of the Howe book. She had discovered it when she was ten, the day she sneaked into the parlor, where access was forbidden to the children because of the many breakable collectibles it housed. She had found it lying alone on a marble-topped table as if it were as holy as the Bible itself. She had spent hours hiding in the parlor and reading the book and falling in love with frontier America. She had admired the forgotten heroes, the Wetzels and the Zanes, and had despised the villains of the time, the Girtys. It had to be THE BOOK.

I never dreamed I'd see another copy of Howe's book. I have to have it.

Careful not to damage the spine, she eased it from the shelf, turned it face up. Joy flooded her face as she slid her palm lightly over the raised image as if she were caressing a newborn kitten.

She opened the book to the title page. *Oh my, yes. It is. It is. It's 1857, Henry Howe and George Tuttle.*

And it's in far better shape than Dad's. Why this one is in prime condition. I'm taking it.

She didn't bother checking the rest of the house. Nothing could match this find. At the front door again, she stopped to pay for the book. Only one of the ladies was at the table.

"I see you found a book," she said. "We're selling hardback books for $1.00 each."

"That's all? Why some of them are worth a lot more. Even this one." She handed it to the lady. "You sure just a dollar is all you want for it?"

The lady looked at it, opened it to the title page, and shrugged. "Why, it's just an old history book. A dollar is plenty. Besides, we have about two thousand books in there."

Debra pulled her wallet from her belly-pack and removed a five. "Since it's for charity, I'd feel better if I paid the one and donated four."

The lady handed the book back to her and took the cash. "That's mighty generous of you. You don't have to do that."

"Well, considering I loved this book when I was growing up and my brother got the family copy, I am happy to contribute to the Boys and Girls Club."

"Thank you," came the response as Debra walked out the door. She had to step aside as several prospective buyers came up the three steps to enter.

She hugged the book as she strolled to her car. All she wanted to do was get home and read, read, read. Re-live those childhood days of Indian wars and frontiersmen and settlers in the Ohio Valley.

At home, she turned on her reading lamp, settled in her leather chair, and propped her feet on the stool. As she settled the book in her lap, it fell open to some middle area. A left-hand page almost stood upright. She laid it over.

An envelope lay between pages 188 and 189. She picked it up, and underneath it lay a newspaper clipping. The heading read *Sam Nielson, Jr., 17, Dies in Car Crash.* She read the clipping, noticed he was survived by his mother, and died on May 17, 1918. *Too young to be in the war. That poor mother.*

She looked at the envelope and saw it was addressed to Mrs. Sam Nielson, Senior. She could not decipher the date stamp or the city of origin.

She glanced inside, saw what looked like a letter, slid it out and unfolded it. A folded bunch of stamps fell out and landed on the floor. She left them lying as she opened the letter. The return address was Washington, D.C. It bore the date May 13, 1918.

Mrs. Nielson must have gotten the letter after he was killed. No wonder she saved it. Her last message from her son.

She read:

Dear Ma, They messed up last Friday at the printing bureau and I got this sheet of stamps out of the trash. The aeroplane is upside down so they can't be used and aren't worth anything, but I thought you might like to have them as a keepsake from my job. Might better keep it a secret, though, because I think I'm not supposed to take things out of the trash bin.

Love, Sammy.

She lifted the stamps from the floor, unfolded the sheet, and stared. A full sheet of Inverted Jennys. Only one other sheet of these was known to exist and it had been cut into pieces.

My God, one of these sold for almost a million dollars. What is this uncut, unknown, sheet worth?

THE GHOST OF MELVIN GREEN

Melvin found himself lying flat on his back on the ground. He lifted his head and looked around. *Oh, yeah, I was walking down to the lake, just crossed the hayfield and through the trees.*

He saw the standpipe at the dam and reminded himself the water level was finally up to normal. Hurricane Marie had dumped twelve inches in two days.

Melvin got up and started toward the pond. Leaves from the four hickory trees littered the field, but his footsteps were silent. And the doe with her six-month-old fawn feeding on acorns under the white oak ignored him. Neither one lifted its head as he approached.

He stopped, looked around, saw a hawk perched on the pine snag. It too ignored him. He turned around. *My god, that looks like me lying there. It can't be me. But that looks like my shirt.*

He approached the body, bent and looked at himself. Blood covering his plaid flannel shirt had run down his side and puddled on the ground.

I've been shot. How can I have been shot and be here looking down at me? Who shot me? Or rather, I must be hallucinating. I'll pinch myself.

Melvin reached his right hand to the back of his left hand and pinched. He felt nothing. He pinched harder. Again, he felt nothing, and even the hand did not appear to have been pinched.

He shivered.

I must be dead. I must be my own ghost. What happened?

A breeze teased the hickory leaves and yellow drifted down. Some settled on the body. *I always loved the hickory leaves in autumn. They are so magnificent against the blue autumn sky.* He looked up to watch the leaves drift across heaven. And tried to remember.

He had left the house. Started out to fish. Carrying his fly rod. *What happened to the fly rod?*

He looked around but did not see it. Remembering flooded him.

I ran up on Wilbur. He was at the pond. Yes, I was leaving the pond, not going to it. I had a string of fish. And met Wilbur. He had his rifle, the same Remington thirty-ought-six the ranger took away from him just last week for night hunting. How did he get it back? He was coming to hunt. Or was he?

He swore he was going to get back at me for catching him the other night. Ranger Marson told me not to chase the culprits, that I would get hurt. Well, Wilbur didn't hurt me then. In fact, I didn't know he knew I was the one who got his tag number and sent Marson after him. He must have shot me and taken my fly rod.

He must have figured it out. And came out here looking for me.

Nobody knows where I am. Nobody will miss me.

The ghost of Melvin Green sat on a log and watched a buzzard drift on the wind overhead.

Won't be long before others come. And then the coyotes. I am not going to sit here and watch them eat me. I'm going hunting for Wilbur.

Melvin rose and began to walk through the trees toward his house. The wind behind him lifted him and he realized he could fly as easily as he could walk.

He passed his home, crossed the highway, drifted toward the crossroads and four stores that passed for town, and continued over the pastures toward Wilbur's ten-acre country estate.

He willed himself to land in Wilbur's yard. No one was around. Wilbur's gray Nissan pickup was gone.

Melvin settled on the Green Egg cooker and waited.

More than an hour passed before the Ford pickup rumbled and rattled into the yard. Wilbur backed down his driveway and parked outside the carport. He got out, walked around to the back of the truck and dropped the tailgate open.

Melvin drifted over to see what was in the truck bed. A buck, eight points, except for a four-inch drop tine on the right beam between the ear guard and the adjacent tine. The buck Melvin had photographed numerous times on the trail camera in his own yard.

Bastard killed my yard pet after he killed me. My mama was right, he is a self-made revolving bastard, a bastard any way you turn him, but he made himself a bastard—his mama isn't to blame.

Melvin spoke, "You..." And stopped. *My god, I can talk.*

Wilbur looked up and glanced side to side. "Must be the wind," he muttered.

"Noooo. Not the wind."

"What in hell is that?"

"It's me, Wilbur. Melvin is back."

Wilbur dropped his skinning knife and ran under the carport. He stopped at the closed kitchen door and looked around.

"You can't run, Wilbur. I can follow you."

Wilbur jerked the door open, scrambled inside, and slammed the door closed. Melvin drifted through the screen and the wood and stood in the kitchen where Wilbur was pulling a beer from the fridge.

"I told you. You can't run, Wilbur."

Wilbur dropped the beer bottle. It broke and beer ran over the floor.

"Oooohhhhhhhh," Melvin whispered. "Shaaaaammmeee."

Wilbur ran out to the carport, scrambled into the truck and drove off. The deer slid off the tailgate and landed on his right side.

Melvin perched on the upper, left antler beam and waited for Wilbur to return.

Darkness fell. A car drove into the yard, its roof light bar flashing red and blue, its headlight beams on the front door. The lights remained on as the driver and passenger got out.

One said, "I don't know what we'll find here. Wilbur says Melvin Green is out here somewhere threatening him. But Melvin's truck isn't here. No lights on. Wilbur shore acted crazy."

The other officer said, "Let's go out to Melvin's. If he's not at his house, he'll be at his pond."

"At night?"

"Yes. He's got power at the pond. I've fished with him. He likes to fish at night, especially in summer. When it cools down. He's got a sink and a pump to pull up lake water to wash off his cleaning stuff and his hands. Everything anyone would want to clean fish."

They reentered the car. Melvin perched on the light bar. Unaware of the roof-top rider, they drove toward Melvin's home.

The officers did not stop at Melvin's house—no lights on, and Melvin's truck parked beside the front porch. The deputies headed across the field, entered the woods, and as they entered the meadow with the pond, they spotted two coyotes snarling over the body. The driver turned on the siren and sped toward the coyotes. The critters fled.

Melvin watched and listened as the deputies studied the body.

"Looks like he's been dead several hours. Howcome Wilbur said Melvin was just at his house? The man's crazy. He must be the one who shot Melvin. Let's get Sheriff Bill out here."

"Yeeeessssssss," Wilbur sighed aloud. "He did."

"Didja hear that?" the driver said. "I'd of sworn I heard Wilbur talking to us."

"Naw, it was just the wind. I'll stay here to keep the coyotes off. You go get Sheriff Bill and one of the detectives."

The driver left. The remaining deputy walked to the edge of the woods and settled on a pine stump. Wilbur wanted to warn him he was going to get redbugs but when he tried to speak, he couldn't even groan.

Melvin drifted to his body, gave up his own ghost and became just dead.

THE FRAUD DEPARTMENT

Howie leaned back in his chair and laid his feet on his desk top. Tomorrow he would retire. He'd had a great run and since he was in charge of the Fraud Department no one was out there to investigate him or his doings or for that matter, any of his non-employees.

And the simpleton he had hired to replace him wouldn't have the sense to investigate the present or future, much less the past.

Being best friends from childhood with the newly elected mayor and having extensive computer skills had enabled his operation to begin twelve years ago. "We need a department in our city government to investigate fraud. Remember, over in Tickleboro last year they caught a fella in maintenance who was skimming city money by claiming personal purchases were for the city. And I would have found that out before the guy had stolen millions."

So his buddy the mayor requested city council to create the new department. The council agreed. The Fraud Department was established, and Howie was hired.

Howie's first step was to visit graveyards over in Alabama and Mississippi to search for markers. He needed the names of children born in 1950s and dead within a few months. He found enough to staff his department. His computer skills enabled him to find the Social Security number for each child. He would be sure income taxes were paid and the IRS would have no reason to question his future employees.

His office, with the latest in computers, became his research station and his lifeline to wealth.

He investigated everyone in the company, and over his tenure of twenty-two years, he uncovered a half-dozen schemes with the aid of his seven non-employees. Each had a checking account, no two at the same bank—three in Macon, one in Dublin and three in Warner Robins. Howie went to each bank only once, to open the accounts. He never returned to the banks or even the neighborhood of any of them.

Nobody investigated Howie. Not even Personnel when he brought in the paperwork for a new employee, and no one in Personnel saw the new people. Paychecks went to direct deposit.

He had very little staff turnover. Why should anyone leave when their records in personnel indicated excellent work and promotions came with pay raises? Alan stayed on for seven years and no one noticed when he resigned. His work was that of two men, Howie explained to Personnel, and he then hired James and Willie. Why not two instead of just one was Howie's idea. He let James find a job in Atlanta after ten years.

Fourteen years into his operation, Howie hired the nephew of a bureaucrat he'd become friends with over the years. The boy was not bright, but his job was to answer the phone because, Howie explained to Personnel, he and his staff had to be out of the office investigating all over the city's complex of offices.

The Tomorrow Howie had worked for finally came.

Howie retired with no fanfare. Everyone was happy. The Inside Cop as he was called, was gone. The bureaucrat's incompetent nephew took over the job. Everyone was now safe to return to the old ways of skimming with the knowledge they would never be investigated or caught.

Howie transferred his seven employee's retirement accounts into joint accounts with himself and then to single accounts in his name alone.

He headed South, to the islands, purchased a small house overlooking the beach, and enjoyed his retirement. He never looked at a computer again.

JAKE, THE TURKEY HUNTER

When he first learned that a year-old turkey gobbler was called a *jake*, Jake Warren had laughed. But he no longer laughed. Seven years of turkey hunting, and he hadn't even been close to killing a jake, much less a mature gobbler.

His wife threw him out of the house every year in February when he began to practice calling turkeys. The mouth calls choked him from the first time he tried to use one, so he concentrated on the slate and box calls.

In his back yard, he called up crows and frightened the smaller birds into flight. He considered himself competent with both by the opening day of his first turkey season, but for six years every time he heard a gobbler sound off or spotted one in the distance and tried to call, his hands shook, his heart almost burst through his rib cage, saliva tried to choke him, and the only sounds he was able to make were screeches that warned the gobbler a hunter was nearby.

No bird came within one hundred yards, three times the range of his shotgun.

This year, he swore he was not going to get the shakes. He was going to get some jakes. Or at least one. Maybe if he just put out a few decoys near where the birds roosted and waited, at least one would spot the decoy, be fooled, and come in close enough for him to take home a trophy. He chuckled at the thought, even a jake would be a trophy.

Preparation was the answer, too, he decided. Get to the woods before the season, scout the land for scratching signs and check out roosting sites. Listen for gobblers and get over his turkey season version of buck fever. He began his spring vacation two days before the season opened.

Thursday morning was cold and wet. Not a gobble to be heard, but Jake was not to be denied. He walked the woods, up and down hills, slopping through ditches that were usually dry but today flooding from the downpour. Two hours of wet, and he headed back to the camp house to dry off and warm up.

He lit the wood-burning stove in the cabin, shucked down to his skivvies and put on dry clothes. No extra boots, so he removed them and set them near the stove without regard to the effects the heat would have on the leather.

Friday morning, he scrambled up when the alarm woke him well before first light. Breakfast was a cup of instant coffee and a bear claw. In full camo and with his .12-gauge automatic Remington in hand, he headed out. The season might not start till tomorrow, he thought, but just let a bird come close enough and he'd take it, law or no law, season or not. *Nobody else'll get here till well after dark tonight, so none of them would know if I shoot a bird a little early.*

He set out from the cabin and took the path toward the patch of clover they had planted last Labor Day. Surely the birds would roost near it since clover was one of their favorite foods. Chufas were better, but that field was a half-mile over the ridge. He'd check the clover patch first.

Spring was trying to slip into the woods. He passed an old house site that was marked by a crumbling chimney standing like a ghost in the rising mist. Scattered clumps of daffodils brightened the otherwise barren ground. He thought he might pick a few when he headed home. Maybe a handful of flowers would appease Ginger for his long absences to hunt. He grimaced. She had never once complained about his time away or the cost of everything.

Nothing in the clover patch except deer droppings he managed to step in as he crossed the field. *Hafta clean up my boots when I get back to camp. Gonna need a stick or screwdriver to pry the mess out of the grooves in the soles.*

The sun threw long fingerlike shadows of the oak limbs across the meadow. He had barely reached the other side when a gobbler sounded off toward the creek to his left. Jake froze in mid-step, realized he was about to lose his balance, and put his upraised food down. His heart rate increased. His hand gripping the shotgun began to shake. Sweat erupted over him, ran down his back and down his face.

Another bird called back. A raucous yelp. Hen or jake? Gotta be a jake. Got to be.

He dropped to the ground, wiggled on his butt to the base of a nearby pine, pulled his knees up and laid the forward stock of the shotgun on his left palm resting on his knee. He pulled the weapon tight to his shoulder.

Damn bird come in this field, it's a dead bird, season or not.

A bird came into the field to his left. *Tom or hen? No, not a gobbler, no red head. Blue head. Oh my god, it's a jake, it's got a beard. Scrawny, but a beard. Damn if I'm gonna pass this up.*

The turkey dropped its head and pecked away on clover leaves. Jake took a deep breath and lined up the shotgun bead on the bird's head, and waited.

Seventy yards away. Each minute he waited became Eternity. A stick under his butt became a log of stobs. Mosquitoes discovered his warmth and buzzed him. He had not put on a face mask and the mosquitoes began their feast. He dared not swat them. He was gonna get this bird no matter what.

Fifty yards. The turkey lifted its head and checked the surrounds. Looked back. Another bird entered the field. Bird One clucked, and the newcomer answered.

Jake's buck fever increased in intensity. He swallowed his salvia and hoped the birds didn't hear him. He knew they could see his eyes at a hundred yards if he blinked. And see his bare face if they even looked his direction.

Forty yards. Thirty. He pulled the trigger.

The kickback rocked him, but the bird flapped. Jake scrambled to his feet and dashed to the turkey. Stomped his foot on its neck so it couldn't escape. Wings flapped twice and the bird lay still.

Jake's victory shout could have been heard a mile away.

He realized he should not have yelled. He grabbed the bird, ignored the scattering of feathers, and headed back to camp. He passed the patch of daffodils, thought briefly of Ginger, but hurried on. She would be happy he had a turkey and would never know about the flowers he didn't bring her. At the camp house, he stuffed the turkey into a large plastic garbage bag and shoved it behind the truck seat. He gathered up the few items he had brought to camp, stored them in another garbage bag, and threw it into the truck bed.

He headed home, so excited he pounded on the steering wheel. He couldn't wait to show off his success to his wife.

And he suddenly realized he had no idea how to clean a bird.

But he shook his head and laughed. *I'll figure it out. It can't be too hard. Maybe Ginger knows something about it. She buys whole turkeys for holidays.*

He was ten miles up I-20 headed home when he noticed three trucks going the other direction, blue lights flashing. *Looks like law enforcement. Glad they're not on my side. I don't want any traffic stops for any reason.*

In another five miles, however, two trucks came up behind him. One passed, and he noticed the Game &Fish Law Enforcement seal. He laughed. Not after him. Pity whomever they are chasing.

A siren joined the lights behind him. *Uh-uh, now what?*

Jake slowed. The siren and lights stayed behind him. He pulled over and slowed to a crawl. The truck ahead of him also pulled over, as did the one behind him. A third one squealed to a stop beside him.

He rolled down his window and cut off the motor. An officer came up to the driver's door.

"What's going on, Officer?" Jake asked.

"Please step out of your vehicle, sir," the ranger replied. "And keep your hands where I can see them."

"Okay. Sure. But what's the trouble?"

Jake slid off the seat and stood beside the truck. He asked again, "What's going on?"

Three officers surrounded him. The one with gold bars on his collar asked, "Where's the turkey?"

Jake felt as if his insides were falling out through his bottom. He coughed and tried to smile. "What are you talking about? What turkey?"

"We know you have a turkey, sir. Where is it?"

"I don't have a turkey. It's not even turkey season, is it?"

"No, it's not turkey season, but you have a turkey. Where it is?" One ranger dragged the bag of clothes to the tailgate and opened it.

"Nothing here but clothes," he said. "Gotta be in the cab."

"Look, men, I don't know why you think I have a turkey."

The lieutenant explained. "You killed a bird with a tracking device, one that has been part of a scientific study for three years. So we know it's in your truck. Besides, you not only killed it out of season, but you killed a rare bearded hen."

THE OLD WOMAN AND THE TEENAGERS

Word was out that she was crippled and couldn't patrol her land as she had for more than forty years. She knew trouble would grow exponentially by deer season, three months away. She determined to be able to get around by then. Meanwhile, let the poachers think she was still laid up.

She rose at 4:30 the opening day of deer season, and after she cooked venison sausage and fried eggs, she donned her hunting clothes and prepared to go poacher hunting. She removed the plug from her Remington semi-automatic shotgun and shoved in four shells. She cranked one into the chamber and added one into the magazine.

She opened her back door onto fog and silence. Sunrise was still a half-hour away and the predawn light was swallowed by the fog. Not even the blue jays were awake to squawk at the morning.

Her right leg ached, but the doctor had assured her walking would not damage the now-healed break unless she stepped into another stump hole. Once was enough, she had assured him.

She began her patrol in her pickup and drove the five-mile road that looped around her two thousand acres. Nobody parked on the shoulder. No gate down. Back at the house, she left the truck and set out on foot down the power line that bisected her land. The gate was locked, but she noticed a second lock had been added to the chain.

Yep, somebody thinks he can sneak in. I'll just see about that.

She strode the edge of the power line. The fog swirled as if it wanted to escape the pull of the earth, but when she topped the first ridge, she was above the fog line. The sun threw pine and oak shadows across her and the opening under the lines.

No sign of poachers. Deer had left a trail where two had kicked moisture from the grass. No sign of human footsteps.

She crossed the first creek and took the old cow path to her right, into the woods, and followed it until the land rose to another ridge. She eased to the ridge top to look over the meadow that ran from the wood line where she stood to the road some 500 yards away. A dozen does, as unafraid as a herd of dairy cows, fed on the over-seeded silage.

Nothing spooked them this morning.

She cut back into the woods and continued north to the next creek. No sign of boots, just a lot of deer tracks, at the crossing. The fourth crossing showed one set of boot tracks, but the mud in the crossing had dried at the track edges.

"Yesterday," she thought.

She turned to her right, toward the road, where there had been no sign of poachers on her predawn ride. From the road, however, she had been unable to see over the twenty-foot-high bank where she had planted red tip and cedars years ago to block poachers from shooting into the pasture from the road. She would have to walk around the bend to see farther down the field, but when she reached the edge of the woods she faced a thick fog. Visibility was no better in the meadow than it had been in the woods.

The wind rose and fog swirled. She glanced to her right and stared. A pile of brush materialized at the edge of the field about fifty yards away. She walked to the opening. The top two strands of the fence were cut, pulled back and wrapped around posts. She stepped over the single strand and cursed under her breath. A station wagon sat parked about forty yards south. Parked since she drove by less than an hour ago. *These suckers are headed to jail and a guaranteed $500.00 fine.*

Once on the road, she trotted toward the car.

Voices reached her. Two male voices. Poachers. Behind her. In the field.

Must have been hidden by the curves and fog.

She hurried back toward the opening, climbed up the bank, eased through the fence and brush and looked into the meadow.

Two men stood with their backs to her only a few feet away. Another, about fifty yards into the field, crept bent over as if searching for tracks. All three had rifles slung on their shoulders.

She eased through the fence and stood at the field's edge. Her camouflage blended her into the background. She un-slung her .12-gauge Remington semi-automatic and held it sideways but with her fingers on the trigger guard. She stepped into the field. Silent as the fog, she walked up to within three feet of the two.

"Fellas, put down those guns. Now."

The two spun around. The business end of the shotgun pointed away from them.

Kids, she thought. Just kids. "Slowly," she said. She stepped closer. One immediately obeyed, un-slung his rifle and laid it on the ground.

"You too," she told the other one. She pushed the shotgun forward, still parallel to herself and the boys.

He un-slung his rifle but instead of laying it on the ground, he pointed it toward her. The end of the barrel almost touched her belly.

The boy moved his finger to the trigger.

"Old lady, you ain't about to tell me what to do." He yelled.

From across the field, the older man called. "Buddy, don't you shoot!"

The boy turned his head, upper body and rifle.

For her, the events were simultaneous:

The boy's finger jerked the trigger

The older man dropped to the ground

A buck rose from his bed in the woods

The bullet hit the buck

The woman slammed the barrel of her shotgun into the shooter's head

The younger boy charged toward his father screaming "Dad," over and over

The shooter dropped the rifle as he collapsed to the ground.

The woman lifted both rifles and swung them over her shoulder. She then pulled out her cell phone and called the sheriff as she hurried toward "Dad" who was rising to his feet.

"You and your boys have to wait. The law is on the way. That one," she nodded toward the boy still laid out on the ground, "faces lots of charges."

In minutes, two patrol cars arrived with sirens screaming and lights flashing. She left the poachers to the deputies and went into the woods to check on the deer she had seen. She hoped it was not the twelve pointer she had captured on her trail camera the past two months.

But it was. She found him, dead, thirty yards from where he had bedded. No longer a trophy, he now was only legal evidence.

A SATURDAY AFTERNOON IN GEORGIA

Bobby recognized the two white men before they stepped out of the car. Mr. Marion in the felt hat he always wore, and the sheriff's brother, that Mr. Sims, who worked for him. Bobby knew they both always toted a pistol.

Bobby was a little scared of Mr. Marion. The old man jumped all over him that time he opened the Frigidaire at the grocery store and saw all those bottles of pee everybody talked about. Everybody said Mr. Marion was wanting to find out who was trying to poison him so he was keeping the pee. Somebody said he tried to get all the doctors in town to test it for poison. Even Dr. Benson. the colored doctor.

Bobby's brother Billy owed Mr. Marion money. Lots of money for a car. Mr. Marion was scary enough, but Sims was worse. There was talk in their part of town that Sims was the one who shot up the honky-tonk.

As they came up the porch steps, Bobby saw the hate in Sims' squint.

"Where's Billy at?" Mr. Marion asked.

"He done gone off to work," Bobby said. He sifted his weight on the porch railing, leaned his weight on his right hand and thought of how far down it was behind him to the ground. If Sims knocked him off the railing, he didn't want to break his head on one of the rocks down there in the weeds.

Howcome I didn't jest get inside when I saw them driving up?

"I came to get my money," Mr. Marion said. "It's way past due. Where does Billy work?"

"You done got the car, Suh," Bobby said. "That pulp wood truck smashed it up."

"You boys still owe for the car. I asked you once. Where does Billy work? Don't make me ask again."

"Naw, Suh. We don't owe nuthin on that-there car. You told us part of what we was paying was for insurance."

"There ain't no insurance. You owe for that car. Where is Billy?" Marion grabbed Bobby's overall bib and shook him.

Sims pulled a pistol from his pocket and pointed it at Bobby.

"He down at the fertilizer plant." His voice trembled.

Marion shoved him as he released his overalls. Bobby grabbed the railing and kept himself from falling backwards.

Two women strode into the yard.

"Whatcha want here, Mr. Marion? Howcome you got a pistol pointed at my boy?"

"I want my money, Lucy. You and this boy and your other boy signed that paper. You own me three hundred dollars."

"We ain't got no three hundred dollars. And you gotcha car back."

"That car ain't no account, Lucy. Your boy smashed it up and you all got to pay for it."

Lucy stepped onto the porch, one arm wrapped around a large paper sack with turnip greens poking out the top. Her daughter Willie eased up behind her. She held a paper sack in both arms as if it were heavy.

Lucy looked at Mr. Marion's chest and said, "Com'on inside, chullin." She strode past him.

Bobby slid from the porch banister. Sims grabbed his arm and shoved him back against the railing. Marion followed the two women into the house; Lucy walked through the living room, into the dining room and then into the kitchen where she set the sack of greens on the cold stove.

"You gonna get me my money?" he asked.

"I ain't got no money," she said. "You needs to git outta here, Mr. Marion."

He pulled the pistol from a holster beneath his jacket, pointed it at her, and shot twice. She collapsed to the floor.

"Mama," screamed Willie.

Bobby charged into the house. Sims ran behind him.

Willie bent over her mother.

Sims shot her.

Willie crawled over to a chest and sat. Marion walked up to her and fired twice into her chest. Bobby ran toward the back door. Marion turned toward Bobby and pulled the trigger again but it clicked on a spent shell.

Bobby disappeared.

"Let's get outta here," Marion said. He and Sims walked out to the porch, looked around and saw no one outside. From next door, a feed sack curtain moved over the window.

"We may be in trouble," Sims said. "Truman sent those FBI men down to Athens about those niggers at Moore's Ford Bridge last year."

"Maybe so, but I don't think we're gonna have any trouble," Mr. Marion said. "This is Georgia, and you know here no white man goes to jail for killing a black-un."

THE PUBLISHING HOUSE AWARD

For the fourth time in less than an hour, the phone rang. *Damn these telemarketers. I'll get rid of this one.*

She lifted the receiver and heard only silence, then a voice, male, said, "Is this Cora? We're calling about the contest you entered."

"I haven't entered any contest."

"Three months ago. You're a winner in the publishers' nationwide contest. Your number was drawn four days ago. We've been trying to reach you. We'll bring your check for ten thousand dollars tomorrow if you're going to be home."

Surprise and joy rose up in her. *Ten thousand. That'll get me out of my credit card debt. I spent hours filling out their forms and sending in the junk last year. I thought that contest was over with. Maybe not. I bet hundreds of people gave up with all those stickers you had to find and glue here and yonder.*

"Oh, I am going to be home. What can you tell me about it? Will you bring the flowers and all that too? But how can I be surprised if you've told me I won?"

"Well, we don't normally tell people they win before we show up, but we've tried to reach you every day for more than a week. Two more days and we would have gone to the second-place person and made whoever that is the winner."

More than a week? They just drew my number four days ago. Oops. Something's not right. I bet. . . I'll go along with them and then call Jim.

"I'm so glad I'm here. I just got back from vacation. A trip I really couldn't afford. Now I can pay off the trip and breathe easy for a while."

"Now I must tell you the check is on the Bank of America. Do you have one near you?"

"Why yes, one opened up not three blocks from me a year ago. I drive by it every time I go to the grocery. I can open an account with them with the check. Oh, I do hope you can be here before three o'clock. They close at four, so I want to be there before they close and open my account. Do you know what time tomorrow afternoon?"

"It'll be between two and three. Let me ask you, however, can you afford the insurance?"

"Insurance?"

"Yes, we have to be sure we have the right person. So we ask for identification. You do have a driver's license?"

"I've had one of those for fifty years! Not a problem. What's the insurance for?"

"It's to ensure we have the right person. In case something happens, it covers our insurance company's fees if someone else claims to be you and we have to have the lawyers sort it out."

"I see. Okay. How much is that?"

"It's only two hundred dollars, but we have to have cash."

"I can't give you a check?"

"I wish I could accept your check, but the insurance company requires cash. I hope you understand. It's their policy."

"Okay. I understand. Give me a call a little before you arrive so I can be sure I have my hair combed in case you take pictures."

He laughed. "Of course. We'll see you around two tomorrow." He hung up.

She returned the handset to the cradle, waited a minute and lifted the receiver to call her brother. "Jim, I need some help here tomorrow." She explained the conversation she had just had.

"I'm on duty tomorrow, but I'll come by at noon and stay until the man comes with the check. I'll get Gary to come with me. I don't like the idea of some stranger getting into your house as if he's a friend. Might be a burglar. Did he give you a number to call?"

"No, and I didn't think to ask him for a number till he hung up."

"I'll check with fraud here and see you tomorrow."

Tomorrow came, and so did Jim.

"You got us a tuna salad sandwich?" Jim asked at noon as he entered her house, with Gary tagging behind him. Both wore civilian clothes with a summer jacket covering their shoulder holsters and badges.

"Come on in the kitchen and we can sit and eat."

They had not reached the kitchen when the doorbell rang. Cora looked at Jim. "That can't be him already. Come on with me to the door."

Jim said, "Gary, stay in the kitchen. I'll go to the door with her."

As she opened the door, Jim eased behind it to be hidden from the visitor. An olive-skinned man in a suit stood on her stoop. He held a briefcase in his left hand.

"Can I help you?" she asked.

"Miss Cora? We talked yesterday. May I come in? I have your check." He extended his right hand as if to shake, but Cora had already stepped back to give him room to enter.

"Yes, of course. I'm so excited. Did you bring a camera man?" She looked around him to her yard, empty except for her car and one parked on the street in front of her house.

A glance to her left showed a number of cars parked near Beatrice's and she wondered if Beatrice were having her book-club luncheon.

"No, I'm afraid not. We take the camera only to present the grand prize of one hundred thousand dollars. Yours is ten thousand."

"Oh, I had hoped to have my picture taken. Well, come on in." She paused, turned to face inside and continued. "Jim? Jim, where are you? Come meet this nice man."

"I would have been right here with you, Sis, if you hadn't slammed the door back into my face." He extended his hand to the visitor. "I'm Jim, her brother. Let's go to the kitchen and sit down and visit a minute or two."

"Well, I need to move on. I have four other deliveries to make this afternoon. I need just to collect the insurance fee and give you the check."

"I have the cash in the kitchen. Come on in."

She walked toward the hall, down it and into the kitchen. The visitor followed her and Jim brought up the rear.

"This is my boyfriend, Gary," she said and pointed to him. Gary smiled, stepped up to the visitor and extended his hand. "I had to be here. This is all she's talked about since yesterday. I'm Gary Nichols and you are—?"

"Oh, my name is not important. I am just the messenger."

Gary stepped back and leaned against the wall by the back door.

"I really do want to know your name," she said. "You are not just a messenger; you have become a friend."

He shrugged. "I'm Richard York. My parents were from Pakistan. I changed my name so Americans wouldn't think of me as a terrorist." He smiled.

"I have your check here," he said. He set the briefcase on the table and removed a folder. Her name was written in red across the front with a Sharpie. He opened it, pulled a cashier's check from under a paper clip and handed it to her.

She smiled and stared at the check. Bank of America. Cashier's check.

"Oh, I can't believe this. Ten thousand dollars!"

She reached to the table and lifted the stack of twenty-dollar bills. "Here's your two hundred for the insurance. Do I get some sort of certificate about the insurance? You know, to show I paid my share?"

"Oh, no, you don't need it. The insurance is to protect my company against any suit. Well, I must be going along."

Jim stood in the doorway to the hall. Gary stood erect and in front of the kitchen door.

"I don't think you're going anywhere for a few minutes, Mr. York," Jim said. "Just take a seat while we sort things out."

"What do you mean, sort things out? What's to sort out?"

"First of all, you come in here with no identification, give her ten thousand dollars in a check in exchange for two hundred dollars cash. Seems a bit fishy to me."

York threw the cash onto the table and reached for the check in Cora's hand. She jerked her hand back. "Oh, no, this is mine now." She stepped toward Gary.

Jim said, "Don't we have some visitors outside? Want to let them in?"

Gary opened the door and women began to enter.

"Get out of my way," York demanded and lunged at Jim.

Jim blocked him and said, "I think you better just stay put, mister." He pulled his jacket back to reveal his holster and the badge attached to his belt.

Jim nodded toward Gary. "He's a cop too."

Fourteen women lined up against the kitchen wall.

York collapsed onto a chair.

"Remember them? They each have one of your useless checks. Welcome to Georgia, Mister York. I hope you like orange outfits. And remember, we serve eggs fried in bacon grease and also bacon for breakfast every day in our jails."

THE TELEGRAM

The thin air mail letter lay alone in her mailbox. Her hands trembled as she pulled it out and looked at it. At least it had a soldier's return address and was not from the Department of the Army.

She ripped it open and sat on the curb to read.

"Darling, the operation is over and I'm coming home. Call the preacher. Should be home in less than a week. They tell me I won't have to come back. You know about D-Day from the news. I'll tell you all about the past three years when I get home. Love and kisses."

After more than three years of no news, no letters, no nothing, she knew he was alive. Not a word since the two officers came for him the day before their wedding and he had to leave immediately to the war. Romance had come and gone and left her pregnant and in disgrace in 1942. If she had not gone to that USO dance she would not have met him, not have gotten pregnant and not had the wonderful daughter who looked just like her father.

Disgrace or not, she was delighted with her daughter and grateful her parents had finally come around.

When he left his last words had been, "I'll write when I can. But I know they're going to send me behind the lines. If you don't hear from me, don't worry." He had laughed then and said, "Unless a pair of officers comes to the door to tell you I'm dead."

All she knew about his military duties were that he excelled in German and French—with parents who taught languages, he had grown up speaking English, German and French at home on alternating days. His blond hair, blue eyes and pale complexion were perfect for undercover spying in Germany.

She lay her head in her palms and wept with relief.

"Mary, are you all right?" Jeri Jenkins asked. Mary had not heard the elderly lady at her own mailbox.

She looked up. "Oh, Mrs. Jenkins, he's coming home." She held up the letter. "He's out from wherever he was and is coming home. He said to call the preacher."

Jeri smiled. "Oh, Mary, I'm so glad for you. I know how worried you've been. Just like me. I got a letter today too. If I didn't hear from Jack at least every couple of weeks I'd be afraid he was lying dead somewhere. At least he made it through D-Day and is now somewhere in France. He said he was looking forward to Paris."

Mary smiled. "He used to tell me how his father loved to sing how can you keep them down on the farm after they've seen Paree."

They laughed.

"Did he say when he might be home?"

"No. Just that he was through with his work with the war in Europe." She stood up. "You know, at least he won't have to go to the Pacific. He doesn't know a word of Japanese."

"What does language have to do with it?"

"Oh, I couldn't tell you or even my parents. I didn't dare. He was probably not even supposed to tell me, but he was in Germany as a spy. His German was perfect, even to no American accent. I better get on back inside with Melissa."

"You call me when he gets home and I'll sit with her while you two go out," Jeri said.

Two days later, she received another soldier's mail. He would be leaving for London and then New York in four days, would fly to Atlanta and catch the Trailways to Tickleboro and see her soon.

Inside the house, she went to her phone to call Jeri with the news. She dialed and looked out at the street while she waited for Jeri to answer. As she watched an army vehicle drove by slowly down the block, turned around and pulled into her driveway.

She dropped the phone. It thunked onto the floor. She covered her face with her hands and stared in terror as two officers climbed out of the car and approached her front door.

The doorbell rang. In the bedroom she cried. She sucked in a deep breath, wiped her face and went to the door.

Both officers removed their hats. "Mrs. Jenkins?" one asked.

"Oh my god. He's okay. But Jeri. Oh Jeri—'"

IT HAPPENED NEXT DOOR

Midnight, too hot to sleep, and Jennifer sat on her front porch, a glass of homemade muscadine wine in her hand resting on the arm of her oak rocker made by her grandfather. She and the chair had celebrated becoming seventy-nine only two weeks ago.

She wondered if the Hershey's would be home tomorrow. She missed them, but was glad they had left their Jeep Cherokee in the driveway and their living room light on. The combination gave the impression that someone was home.

Her house was dark, no lights to attract July insects. A citronella candle burned behind her to keep the mosquitoes at bay.

The moon sat mid-sky and lit the moving clouds with its own halo. The summer night was so warm she kept mopping sweat from her face. Summer or not, it was way too hot for early July. A tad of winter would be nice right about now.

She laughed as she remembered years ago when snow surprised the town and all the neighborhood children turned the day into a sledding event on their hillside. Nobody had sleds, but they had used cardboard boxes from the local A&P as makeshift sleds. She smiled as she remembered the time she and Anne Williston, now Mrs. Dave Hershey, had tumbled down the hill together when their cardboard bumped a fallen limb.

She heard a crash, like glass breaking, and glanced over at their house. A shadow moved across the living room window. Something else crashed, and the light went off.

She ran inside and dialed "operator" on her rotary desk phone.

"Operator."

"Hi, Peggy. This is Jennifer. As if you didn't know. Anyhow, I need the sheriff. Somebody's broken into the Hershey's house."

"Oh, my goodness," Peggy replied. "Are you all right? You aren't going over there, are you? You might get killed. Or kidnapped, like we heard about that lady over up north in Atlanta when she went to investigate something going on in her neighbor's house. You stay home, you hear?"

"I have no intention of investigating myself. Just put me on to Carol at the sheriff's."

"Sure. Just hold on."

"Sheriff's office."

"Carol, this is Jennifer. I hate to bother you, but you know the Hershey's are out of town this weekend, and something is going on in their house."

"What do you mean? Should I send a deputy out?"

"That's just it. I'm not sure. They left their living room light on, and I was sitting on my front porch when I saw a shadow move across the light. Through their window, of course. And then I heard a crash and the light went out. I think they have a burglar."

"Okay, I'll send out a couple of deputies. Don't you go over there. Do you have a key?"

"Yes, have them stop here and I'll give them the one I have. I can't imagine what's going on. I hope it's not a burglar."

Jennifer went out and sat on her rocker on the front porch. Within five minutes, a sheriff's car pulled up in front, and she scooted down her sidewalk to meet the deputy who slid out of the passenger seat.

"Hi, Andy," she said. "Here's my key to the Hershey's house. The kitchen light came on after I talked to Carol and it just went out. It's set to come on when one of them walks in and stays on only as long as someone is in the kitchen."

"We'll check it out. You might need to stay inside, just in case."

"Okay," she replied and headed back to her front door.

Andy suggested to his partner that they walk over to the other house rather than pull up in front. If there were a burglar inside, better to surprise him than warn him and have him flee or shoot at them.

Andy unlocked the front door and faced darkness complete except for a narrow bar of light from the street light two houses away. He turned on his flashlight and looked over the hallway. No sign of anyone.

"I'll check out down here," he said. "You want to take the second floor?"

Russell said, "Okay. Be careful" He pulled out his pistol, and with the flashlight in one hand, his .38 Special in the other, he crept up the stairs.

Andy tried to swallow, but his mouth was too dry. When he reached for his pistol, his hand shook. He shivered and worked his jaw to make the saliva flow. Get a hold of yourself. He pulled out his pistol and turned to the room on his right. He eased to the doorway, stood behind the jamb and moved the flash beam across the room. Nothing but furniture, an empty bird cage and a broken lamp on the floor.

Somebody's been here. Probably stole the bird and busted the lamp. Probably gone by now. God, I hope so. I don't want to get shot.

Behind him he thought he heard something. No sound of footsteps. But he felt the air move. Someone was there, easing around, stirring the air. *God don't tell me ghosts.* He turned, but only the empty hallway lay before him. He swept the hall with his flashlight but found no sign of danger. Just the coat rack and the mirror that reflected his flashlight. He sighed and let out his breath.

He went to the front door and closed it. Maybe the wind was coming in the door.

He stood a moment and listened to Russell's footsteps overhead. The floor creaked with each step he took. His flashlight illuminated the upstairs hallway a moment and moved on. *Thank God there's nobody in the house.*

Andy stepped across the hall and entered the dining room. As he did so, something grabbed his left shoulder, stabbing him through his uniform and jacket.

He ducked and tried to spin, but the grip did not loosen. He pointed his pistol over his shoulder and fired.

Feathers flew as the family's escaped parrot fell dead.

———————————

Thanks to Pat Blanks for the idea for this story.

THE REAL ESTATE AGENT

Edwina stepped out of her car, checked her pocket for the smart key, locked her purse inside, and pulled a house key from her other pocket as she strode up the walkway to the door. This had been the strangest sale she had ever received: A key in the mail, with a note that said, "Just sell it. I'll be back in touch for where to send the money. Message me at –"

She inserted the key into the lock and as she turned it, a voice behind her ordered, "Do not move a muscle or you're dead."

She felt something blunt and cold against her neck.

"What do you want?" she stammered. "You can have my car. The smart key is in my pocket."

"I don't want your car. I want you to turn around real slow and you're gonna walk down the street in front of me like we're good friends. I'll keep this here pistol pointed at you all the time. You may not feel it, but it'll be close enough you'll be dead if you try to run or do anything smart. You got that?"

"Yes." Her voice broke. She turned slowly and felt him behind her all the time, felt the pistol move from her neck to her back and then ease away.

"Don't even think of trying to look back at me, ya' hear?"

Her voice didn't work. Her tongue was cemented to the roof of her mouth.

"I said, you hear me?"

She nodded. She moved her tongue around, curled it up against the roof of her mouth to try to get some moisture to flow.

They approached a white Toyota van. She read the tag number and repeated it over and over in her mind. *Maybe if I get out of this, that tag number will help get the kidnappers,*

"Stop," the voice ordered. She turned the tag number into a musical pattern to help her remember.

The street was empty. No one in sight.

"Don't move. I'm gonna put a pillow case came over your head so you can't see where we go." The material slid over her. She continued the mantra of the tag number. If I can't see them, can't ID them, there's a chance they won't kill me.

"Get in the car," he ordered.

"I can't see."

"I ain't taking it off your head. Reach out here," He took her left arm and put her hand against the open door. "Turn to your left and feel for the seat."

She followed instructions, felt the seat, and climbed in.

"Fasten that-there belt," he ordered.

It was easy to feel the seat belt and secure it.

She heard a door open to her left and the driver get in. She heard him click the seat belt. And felt the car shift slightly as the second man got in behind her. She tried to mentally figure where they were going, but after four turns, she was lost.

They drove for miles on the expressway, but she wasn't sure if they were going east or west. Or how far.

They exited, drove another ten minutes, and finally stopped.

Her door opened. "Get out," a new voice ordered.

She obeyed. A hand seized her arm. "Come on."

She walked on dirt. "Where are we? What do you want?"

"You know damn well where you are, Alice," the voice said. "And you know you're getting your final reward."

"Alice? Who's Alice? I'm Edwina."

The pillow case was jerked off her head.

A stranger stared at her.

"Who in hell are you?" he asked

"Edwina. The real estate agent hired to sell the house."

"Well, this is your lucky day. Have a nice walk home," he said, turned and walked to the car. He got in and they drove off.

She felt in her pockets. They had not taken anything, and she used her cell phone to call 911. At least she remembered their tag number.

And she reckoned she better warn Alice—if she could only find a way to reach her.

RETURN FROM THE UNDISCOVERED COUTRY

Stuart Littleton IV was not known for his art although he had sold three paintings: One to his father, one to his father-in-law and one to his sister. Today he was celebrating the sale to his sister. He was spending the three hundred dollars for supper with his wife, Vivian, at the Bacchanalia in Atlanta.

Just as dessert was being trundled up on a cart, he began to feel something strange in his mouth, as if it were swelling. He mentioned it to Vivian, and her eyes widened. "Gawd, Stu, you shouldn't have eaten that shrimp. Remember last time? You broke out in hives. We better get you to the hospital."

They skipped dessert and she drove. At the hospital, she pulled into the emergency entrance, parked alongside an ambulance and scrambled out. Stuart opened his door. An emergency technician heading toward the ambulance took one look at Stuart, grabbed him, shoved him into a wheelchair, and hustled him inside.

The EMT went directly to the registration window, said, "We have an anaphylactic patient. Get a doctor STAT."

In less than a minute, Stuart was in a treatment room. Vivian was told to wait outside and to move her car from the ambulance bay. She didn't want to do either, but common sense told her to obey the hospital staff. She ran out, moved her car into the visitors' parking lot, and ran back to the waiting room. Not an empty chair, so she paced. Others looked at her, still clad in party finery, high heels and distress. Most of the others wore only street clothes or whatever they had on when they were injured or began vomiting. The waiting room held a faint odor of old vomit and sweat.

In the treatment room, Stuart looked down and realized he was floating against the ceiling of a strange room and looking at himself laid out on a table. A doctor and a nurse hovered over him.

I sure do look bad. White as the sheet I'm lying on. I must be dreaming about this floating business. But what's going on? Last I remember is eating those wonderful shrimp and my mouth swelling up and Vivian driving me to the hospital.

Oh, gawd, maybe I'm dead. Maybe I'm on my way to wherever we go when we die. But if I'm dead, what are those two people doing? Oh my, the lady has got a scalpel. She's cutting my throat.

I don't feel anything. If she's really cutting my throat, I would have to feel it. And see it. See them. My eyes are wide open. But the me down there doesn't see the me up here in the ceiling. I just see me laid out down there. And why do those two people glow? A light shines around them like they have some inside electricity pulsing in them.

Here come two more people. Funny, they don't have any light around them. Must not be special like the first two.

Now what are they doing? Sticking a tube in the hole in my throat. They sure look intense. And sound it.

"We're about to lose him. Get the paddles. STAT." The doctor shouted and began to rip Stuart's shirt off.

A three-hundred-dollar shirt and he tears it apart. Howcome he didn't just open up the buttons?

A non-glowing person grabbed something from a cabinet. The doctor grabbed two paddles, slapped one on Stuart's chest and the other to his left side. "Now," the doctor shouted.

Stuart saw himself jerk and spasm. "Again," the doctor shouted.

Stuart spasmed again.

And stared up at the doctor who bent over him.

"He's back," the woman shouted. "Thank God."

The man asked, "How do you feel, Mr. Littleton?"

"My throat hurts. What happened?"

"You came into the emergency room with an anaphylactic reaction to shrimp. We almost lost you. Our usual treatment didn't work—you reacted to it. Your heart stopped, and we had to shock it back and open your throat with a tracheotomy. You'll be fine now. But we'll keep you here for a couple of days.'

"You glowed," he said. "I saw you glowing."

The nurse and doctor looked at each other and shrugged. The doctor said, "You must have been dreaming while you were unconscious."

Stuart wanted to say no he wasn't dreaming, he was watching it all from the ceiling, but thought if he did tell them, they would think he had lost his marbles while he was out. *Maybe I just died and didn't have time to go to hell or heaven before they woke me up. I won't say another word.*

With a heart monitor attached and oxygen pumping directly into his throat, Stuart was moved to the intensive care unit. Three days later, he was home with his neck stitched up and bandaged. And with orders to take it easy, stay home, no work for two weeks, and then back to the cardiologists for follow-up.

That night, he dreamed about a Confederate soldier and a battle. The young soldier was frightened as the armies clashed. He was on the front line, behind a low mound of fresh dirt. Sweat rolled stark lines through the dust on his face. His blue eyes squinted into the sun. His rifle shook as he shouldered it and fired.

The Rebel screamed and fell back, his left arm spurting blood. The soldier next to him dropped his weapon and grabbed the injured man, pulled him away from the breastworks, and gripped the injury with both hands. Another soldier hurried over, wrapped a strap just above the injury and the two men helped the injured soldier away. Fog descended and Stuart's dream drifted away with the fog.

Stuart awoke, the image of the injured man vivid.

I'll draw him. I haven't hit a lick at my art since I got home. That face. It's so vivid. I can even see his uniform, his firearm, the carving on the stock, the emblem on his cap.

Stuart crawled out of bed although he had been told to stay abed for about a week and then return to the doctor for follow-up. But he had no intention of losing the image in the dream. It was far too exact to lose.

At four a.m., his wife Vivian was dead asleep. He eased out of bed and wearing only his tighty-whities and without donning a robe or slippers, headed to the room set aside for his artwork.

When Vivian roused three hours later, she found him placing the finished acrylic against the wall. "What the hell are you doing?" she asked.

"Oh, and good morning to you to," he said, but grinned. "I had a dream like never before. I saw this man in the dream and when I woke up I had to paint him. "

She looked at the picture, folded her arms and studied it. "You got so much detail. The injured arm, the cap, the sweat, the agony. But especially the eyes. It's as if he's here, in the room with us, looking at us and pleading for help. It's the best you've ever done."

She turned to him, opened her arms, and wrapped him in a light hug. "I love you, Stuart. And I love the picture, but I'm gonna fix your breakfast and then you go back to bed. Remember, doctor's orders."

"I love you too, Viv, and I don't what I'd have done without you. And I am tired, so an after-breakfast nap will be good. Would you do me a favor, though? I think I need more art materials. I have the feeling I'm going to want to paint more."

While she fixed breakfast, he made his list and while he napped, she went to the local art supply store, purchased everything on his list, and placed his supplies in his workroom.

He slept four hours and awoke with a start, his mind filled with the image of a man in overalls, a straw hat, brogans without laces, a Sears-Roebuck work shirt with the sleeves rolled up to reveal thick hairy forearms. The hands showed years of hard work. Behind the man were a stream, a hillside of autumn colors, and a still.

Yes, Viv got everything I wanted.

He selected the 2'X3' canvas and began to work with the acrylics. Stuart worked rapidly, as if chasing the image of his dream before it ran out of the house.

He painted, not a portrait of the man alone but of the site with the man in the foreground. The man held an ax in his right hand as if he were about to swing it down to bury the blade into a log at his feet.

Vivian passed judgment again. "I don't know which is better. This man's eyes seem to look into my soul. His face tells me his life has been harsh. So thin and angular and tired. With no hope left in his life. And his hands. My lord above, you've even gotten every hair on his hands and his arms. I love it."

She turned from the painting and said, "Stuart, you've got to rest."

"I know, and I am tired. But when I go to sleep, I dream these people. And I have to paint them. It's like I've gotten an order from God or something. It's an obsession I can't walk away from."

Three more days and nights Stuart slept, dreamed, roused himself and painted. As he finished the eighth painting, he placed it against the wall beside the others. He sighed. *I hope that's the last one. I am just too tired to keep on like this. I don't want any more of those dreams. I feel like I'm killing myself.*

Stuart walked into the kitchen and sat down in the breakfast nook. Vivian sat opposite him. "You look almost worse than when you came home," she said. "I think we need to talk to the doctor tomorrow about something to help you sleep and not dream."

The doorbell rang. "I'll get it," Viv said and rose.

Moments later, she returned with Stuart's father, Jackson.

"How ya doing, son?" he asked.

Stuart stood and they shook hands.

"He's wearing himself out with his art," Viv said. "You need to see it. I can't get over the details he's painting. And the people. C'mon. Let me show you."

She led the way to the studio. Jackson followed and Stuart trailed.

Jackson halted two steps into the room and pointed to the portrait of the Confederate soldier. "I didn't know you had a picture of great-grandpa Stuart the first," he said.

"What do you mean? You think that's great grandpa Stuart?" Stuart asked.

"Yes. Him. The soldier. That's a perfect image of him. Your great aunt Savannah on my mother's side has a tintype of him made just before the Battle of Cedar Creek. That's where he lost his arm."

Stuart stood silent. Vivian might understand his dreams. Daddy wouldn't.

But Daddy strode to the large portrait of the moonshiner. "That's my great-uncle Silas on my daddy's side. He was po' as a beggar after he lost all he had to gambling. That's when he took up bootlegging and died rich and mean as a stepped-on snake. Where'd you see his picture? I didn't know anybody in the family had one."

Stuart didn't dare admit he met them in the afterlife, that different people came to visit while he slept. He wondered who would visit next.

THE STAR CHILD
AMERICA'S SUPREME HEROINE

Part I

Dead asleep, April lay on her back in the middle of the meadow while dew settled and the Milky Way wheeled overhead. Moisture soaked her jeans, her denim jacket and the flannel shirt where the jacket lay open. It glistened on her black hair spread over the two-inch-high silage that served as a non-mattress on the firm Georgia red-clay. When light began to push against the eastern horizon, she stirred and shivered.

Gads, I'm cold. She wrapped her arms across her chest, opened her eyes and realized she was seeing a dawning sky, not her bedroom ceiling.

Shaking with cold and puzzled, she sat up, looked around. The tree line to her left reached naked limbs skyward. She recognized the pine snag where an owl had nested. She was in the hayfield.

I don't sleepwalk. How'd I get here?

Pain roared through her head. She closed her eyes, gripped her head with both hands and tried to remember. Her last remembrances were a crowd, a party, barbecue, cleaning up and taking a lone stroll in her yard to enjoy the quiet after her annual Labor Day party.

I've got on what I wore at the party, so what in the dickens am I doing out here? Did I lie down to watch for shooting stars and fall asleep?

Acid rose into her throat, flooded her mouth. She rolled onto her shoulder and lowered her head as she began to gag. Bile and mucous erupted as her body spasmed. When the gagging ended, she spit what little salvia she could summon, propped her head on her palm, and waited for more to come.

She took a deep breath and eased herself up to sit, propped her elbows on her knees and held her head. Eyes closed, she tried to think through the clouds that covered her memories. Nothing after the guests left and she went outside. *I feel like I'm drunk, but I don't drink. It must be stomach flu. Oh dear gawd, I hope it's not food poisoning. I hope nobody else is sick.*

She tried to stand, felt her legs wobble, and sat back down. She thought of her father, who in his late years had had trouble standing up after they rested somewhere on the farm after long hours of work. She followed his example, got on her hands and knees, put her weight onto her hands, and one at a time, moved from knee to foot. Rear end high, she inched hands up her legs. Her jeans felt damp.

Finally erect, she took a deep breath and tugged her lightweight Sears denim jacket around, held it closed with her hands crossed. Dawn washed out the stars.

Something roared overhead and she looked up, expecting to see a helicopter, but instead saw only light flare overhead and fade eastward into the rising sun as it crossed over the pine hill.

What the hell is that? Looked like a meteor going backwards. Weird.

She began a slow walk toward her house.

Damp cold gripped her. Moonlight glimmered the dew into a white sheet over the field. After a few steps the footing changed. She looked down. She had stepped from the winter silage over-seeding onto almost naked ground. She looked behind her. Middle of the field. *Something's wrong. We over-planted the whole field last week. Why is part so high and some not growing?* Cold shimmered her again. *I'll figure it out after I get warm. I've got to get to the house before I catch my death.*

She scurried up the porch steps, gripped the door knob and turned it. The door didn't open. *I never lock the door unless I'm traveling. And I haven't been anywhere.*

She went to the empty flower pot, lifted it, grabbed the spare key and let herself in.

She reached to turn on the overhead hall light. Nothing. She flipped the switch again. Only a shaft of light from the rising sun slipping through the open door responded.

No lights, no heat. Cats got to be cold.

"Where are you, kitty?" she called. "Kitty? Kitty?" No cat came to her. She picked up the penlight she always kept on the table by the front door and headed for the kitchen.

The house smells funny. Stuffy. Like it's been closed up.

She continued to call the cats as she walked to the kitchen. She opened the fridge for the half-can of cat food and shown the light inside. The fridge was empty.

What the heck is going on?

She turned from the fridge and saw a sheet of typing paper on the counter by the stove. She picked it up, read the handwritten note.

"I tried to reach you, but no answer. I got worried after three days and came inside. No sign of you. I took Major and Sarge to my house. Where have you been? Please call me. After three weeks I cleaned out your fridge and turned off your power and the phone. I am WORRIED ABOUT YOU. Sally. Sept. 28"

Her neighbor, tenant, friend.

Three weeks? What the heck is she talking about? It's Labor Day week. I haven't been gone anywhere. It can't be the twenty-eighth.

April pulled a chair from the kitchen table and plunked down. She closed her eyes and tried to remember. The same images flitted through her mind that she had visualized earlier: Labor Day. The party. The crowd. The cleaning up afterwards. Sally and several friends staying to help. Everyone finally gone. Taking a midnight walk outside to clear out the smells of barbecue and erase the noises of partying.

Nothing else until now, waking up in the hayfield. Cold enough for November.

But I'm cold because of the dew, like it was when I was a kid and slept out on the windrows of hay with just a sheet and nearly froze when the dew fell and I got wet. It's not really cold. It can't be since it's September. It's the dew, and the vomiting. But I feel cold enough for it to be Thanksgiving.

She went to the phone, lifted the receiver, and when she got no dial tone, remembered Sally's note. She grabbed a coat from the hall closet, shoved her arms into the sleeves and headed next door. Good daylight or not, she was going to talk to Sally and find out what had happened, why no food, no phone, no cats, no power and the house locked up.

At her knock, the porch light came on. A shadow moved across the window pane in the heavy oak door and in seconds Sally flung the door wide, pushed open the screen and grabbed her.

"Are you okay? Where have you been? Why didn't you tell me you were going off and I wouldn't have left the kitties so long without food? Are you all right?"

Comfort wrapped itself around her with Sally's embrace.

"I don't know. I can't remember anything after the party except going outside for a few minutes. I just now woke up in the hay field. And about to freeze. How did I get there? I don't remember—"

Two cats bounded into the living room, curled around her legs and turned on their motors. She squatted, rubbed them both, scratched their chins.

"They missed you, April. As much as I did. What were you doing in the hayfield? You got to be kidding, right?"

"I'm not kidding. I have no idea—" She picked up one of the cats and nestled it against her chest. It began to lick her face.

"Last I saw you was at your Labor Day party."

"Well, it's cold for early September."

"You're not okay. It's not September, it's November. You've been gone for almost two months. I'm going to call Dr. Lucy. Something's wrong. You've lost your memory and no telling what's happened to you."

"Come on, Sally. It can't be November. That doesn't make sense. I remember—well, I remember the party like it was yesterday. I just want to go home right now. Just take the kitties home and get the power back on and get some sleep. I'm tired near to falling down."

"I'll call Steve at the EMC. He'll send a lineman over ASAP and he'll be glad to hear you're home."

Sally tugged April to the living room and pushed her down onto the sofa. "Get off your feet a minute while I call."

As soon as she sat, the other cat jumped onto the sofa and curled against her.

Moments later, Sally returned. "Steve's got the crew on the road already. Said give him a half-hour and they'll have it back on. Now you listen to me. Something isn't right. You've been gone for weeks. Sheriff Buford has really searched high and low for you, even called in the FBI and Jim Ridenour and Dana Furry. They stayed in town searching and talking to everybody for days. We've got to call Sheriff Buford and let him know you're home. He'll need to talk to you. If you've been kidnapped or worse—"

Her voice trailed off into silence.

Sarge jumped onto the sofa, pushed Major away, hunched his back, massaged her thighs and purred his contentment. April stroked his back without looking at him, her concentration on Sally.

"I don't think anything bad happened to me. I'd know. I'd remember. I can't believe I've been quote missing for weeks." She made quote marks with her fingers. "It just doesn't seem possible. Will you call Buford? Tell him I'm home and ask him to call Jim and Dana. I don't have the energy now. All I want to do is take the boys home and go to bed." April smiled. "I feel I haven't slept in weeks when I just woke up. Oh. Is there any cat food at the house?"

"You haven't been in?"

"Just long enough to find the power off and see your note is all."

"Stretch out on the sofa here until Steve gets your power on."

April did, and both cats crawled up with her, Sarge curling up on her upper side and Major snugging against her chest. She fell asleep instantly.

Sally woke her an hour later. "Steve's gone and you have power and heat. I'll get the bag of cat food, some snacks for later. You want me to fix you some breakfast before you go home?"

"No, thanks. I can manage. I've got oatmeal unless mice got in." April laughed at the idea of a field mouse managing to invade her home. It was built so tight even an ant couldn't find a way inside.

Sally came back with a grocery tote bag and a small ice chest. "Got the last half of their food bag, plus some goodies for you. I really think you need to see Dr. Lucy today. You're pale as a dead ghost. You've been missing for so long even the cops gave up on you. You've been on TV across the country. You REALLY need to see a doctor."

"Tomorrow. I'll call her tomorrow. I just need to get some rest. I don't know why I'm so tired." She wasn't about to tell Sally about the vomiting and nausea. Sally would insist on taking her right to the doctor's office.

They trudged across the two yards to her house, with Sally toting one cat and the cooler and April carrying the tote bag and with the other cat laid out over her shoulder. Inside, Sally filled the cat water bowl. "I'll call Buford this morning and tell him you lost your memory and when you remembered, you just came home and don't recollect what happened in between time. Is that okay? No one knew anything. God, April, I'm so glad you're back and safe. You go get your nap in, if the cats don't keep you awake."

"Sit a minute, Sally. It's funny, but when I woke up out there, the meadow felt funny, the silage—well, I was surprised it was high and low both. Like part of it had been cut.

"Do you know what's going? Part of the ground is almost bare and part of it is too high for just being planted. Whoa." She paused. "I forgot. It's November. But who cut some of the silage? It ought not be cut till March or April."

"Nobody's been in the hayfield since Richard planted it last September like he always does for you. It's not been cut."

"Well, I was in a part of it that was cut. I'll figure it out tomorrow. I'll see you later today. Thanks so much." She encircled her arms around Sally. "Love you, neighbor. What would I do without you? What would the kitties have done without you?"

"Love you too. Sleep well." She pointed a finger at April and emphasized again, "You call Dr. Lucy, now, you hear?"

"I will. I promise."

As soon as she closed the door behind her, Sally locked the thumb latch, hooked the chain and turned the key in the deadbolt. "I ain't gonna leave this house again till I figure out what happened."

She fed the cats and headed for her bedroom. Five minutes later, she was asleep. When the early afternoon sunlight slid through the west window and touched her eyes, she awoke with the cats snuggled against her. She stretched, breathed deeply, and got up. Her stomach growled and she headed to the kitchen to fix a breakfast before she faced the rest of the day and the mystery of the missing weeks.

Coffee, scrambled eggs and toast. But with her first sips of the second cup of coffee, her stomach revolted. Nausea gripped her. She hurried to the bathroom and threw up. Not just the coffee but the scrambled eggs and grits. After five minutes of heaving and sitting on the bathroom floor with her head hovering over the toilet, she rose, rinsed out her mouth, and went to her easy chair. Both cats jumped up, one on each arm of the chair, and managed to crowd together into her lap. "You two miss me?" They looked up at her, squiggled against each other, purred and curled up. She reared back, closed her eyes, drifted off and dreamed.

When she woke a half-hour later, the dream crept around the edge of her memory. All she could visualize was the night sky from last night—a clear sky with the Milky Way within reach and the bright reversed meteor flying away into the sunrise.

And something about the hayfield. Something was wrong with the silage. "Got to get up, kitties," she said as she gave them a light shove. They dropped to the floor. She locked the door's dead bold when she left the house for the hayfield.

Reckon that's the first time I ever locked the door when I'm just going out to the fields.

The hayfield stretched across acres to the front and side. She walked into the field. And stared.

Crop circles. *Someone cut stupid crop circles in the silage. Must have destroyed at least three acres with those stupid circles. Who? And when? Why didn't Sally hear the machines? She's always home.*

Back inside, she picked up her phone to call Richard about the silage and got no dial tone. She walked next door to borrow Sally's phone. When Sally opened her door, her first words were, "Are you okay? You look paler now than you did a little while ago. Get any rest? Or those cats keep you awake?"

"Oh, I slept fine. And warm." She smiled. "Nothing like a two-cat nap. Beats a three-dog nap any day." She did not mention having upchucked her breakfast—that information would just spur Sally to take the initiative and call Dr. Lucy herself.

"I'm kinda upset. I've got huge patterns cut into the silage. I have to call Richard. It's his crop. I hope it'll recover before spring. May I use your phone? I need to call Richard. And call the phone company. Mine is still out."

But Richard was as shocked as April had been. He welcomed her home but did not question her about where she had been. She was grateful for his respect of her privacy because she had no idea what to tell him.

The telephone people were unconcerned as to why the phone had been disconnected and assured her they would have it reconnected within 24 hours.

"You need to call Dr. Lucy, now," Sally said.

"Okay. Okay, I will."

"Promise?"

"Promise."

But she didn't. Until two days later, when she still couldn't keep food down.

Dr. Lucy demanded she come in at once. "You've been who-knows-where for weeks, and I've been so worried, even when I heard you had come home. I'll see you today, at five, after my other patients. That'll give us all the time we might need."

Two days later, Dr. Lucy called April back to her office to go over the lab results.

"Pregnant? I can't be pregnant!" April shouted at Dr. Lucy. "I can't be. I haven't... I mean..."

Dr Lucy replied, "April, the labs are correct. You told me yourself you were having trouble with nausea in the mornings. Typical morning sickness. That's why I had the pregnancy test. You are definitely pregnant."

"Doctor Lucy, I swear to you, I haven't slept with anybody. I can't be pregnant."

Unless—oh cripes! I can't believe I slept with somebody and can't remember. But I can't remember anything about those weeks.

"You don't remember anything about the seven weeks you went missing?"

April shook her head. "Nothing. Surely if I had—had—" She paused. "I would remember."

The two friends sat and looked at each other a long moment. Dr. Lucy asked, "Do you want to abort?"

"I don't know. I just don't know what to do. I can't think right now. I'm single. I have to run the farm. I don't know what to do. Give me a day or two to decide. I never thought I would approve of abortion. I just—" She shook her head.

"I understand. You need time to get over the shock. Give it time. Days or even longer."

The answer came to her in a dream that night, and dawn found her remembering the words: *You are to name your daughter Cassiopeia Merlina for she will perform many miracles and travel long distances and join the great women of mythology.*

She didn't tell Dr. Lucy about the dream but called her to say she would not abort the child. It was her baby and the unknown father would not be relevant.

The morning sickness finally passed and April began to show her pregnancy.

She was glad she had rented the cottage next door to Sally, for Sally offered to baby sit and to help in any way she could. School mates and friends, then tenant-landlady over the years. She called on Sally to drive her to the hospital when her contractions began and Dr. Lucy delivered her daughter.

"It's a girl," the doctor said.

"Ten toes and ten fingers?" April muttered.

"All looks good and healthy. We'll clean her up and be back."

April was propped up in bed in her private room when Dr. Lucy came in. "She's healthy, April, but a bit of a wonder. At first, I was afraid she might be mongoloid, her skull is different. But she's not. Her skull does not have a cranial seam and it's a bit elongated. And her eyes are large. Otherwise, she's as normal as any baby I've seen. Heart is strong and regular. Eyes as responsive as normal, but they'll be different colors." Lucy chuckled. "All the boys will be chasing her with those mysterious eyes. She just looks a bit different, but all is well, so don't be surprised."

The door opened before April could reply. "Here's your daughter," the nurse announced and placed the infant in April's outstretched arms. The baby's eyes focused on hers and her lips moved.

"She's smiling," April said as she placed the baby to her breast and thought of the calf she had seen as it was birthed and rose on wobbly legs to instinctively stagger to its mother's udder. As her baby suckled, she slid her hand over the blond-haired skull and realized Lucy was right—her head did seem a bit long instead of rounded. "You're sure she's all right?" April asked as she turned her attention back to Dr. Lucy.

"As right as I can be. We'll watch her, but I think there won't be a problem. And it's just your imagination that she's smiling. Newborn babies can't smile."

April didn't contradict Lucy, but knew she had smiled.

The baby finished suckling and looked up at her as if she could read April's mind, see inside her with her odd-colored eyes—one with an off-white iris and one with a gold iris. April had no doubt this time about the smile.

April obeyed the message in her dream and named the child Cassiopeia Merlina. She told Dr. Lucy she would call her Cassie, but did not tell Lucy she feared other children would make fun of the child if they called her Cassiopeia.

Part II

April sat among the honored guests at the MIT graduation. Eighteen-year-old Cassie was graduating with a Ph.D. in astrophysics and biochemistry, and was to introduce the U. S. President Kyle Jenkins who was to receive an honorary Ph. D. and give the graduation speech.

She had heard her daughter's talk several times. Never before had she seen Cassie nervous, but the prospect of introducing the President of the United States had un-nerved the girl and she had rehearsed her speech numerous times. April noticed, however, that as Cassie looked over the crowd, her hands lightly touched the podium and a light smile curled her lip. She was in complete control. While Cassie spoke, April's mind drifted back over the eighteen years since her birth.

Strange years, filled with events that convinced her of Cassie's childhood claim that her home was in the stars.

She had all the written resources and technical educational instruments she desired. And she had the entire farm, 3,000 acres of woodland, hayfields and wildlife any child would hope for. *Huh, more than even a boy would have hoped for.*

She recalled Cassie's journey and search for knowledge. From her first sight of the child, April had known she was different. Very different. At six months, she began to talk, the night April read to her for the first time—when April reached the end and closed the small book, Cassie quoted the story back to her word for word.

At nine months, she corrected the grammar of the TV news reporters.

April began homeschooling her before she was two, and within a year realized she had surpassed anything April could teach her.

For Cassie's second birthday, April bought the best computer she could find. Whatever Cassie saw or heard she did not forget.

Her insatiable appetite for knowledge had led her to the natural world as well as the technical world. She took to the computer as easily as she had to breathing and explored the outside world as if it were created solely for her exploration and pleasure.

April thought back to that night they walked into the hayfield and Cassie pointed toward the Seven Sisters and stated, "That's home. That's why you named me Cassiopeia."

"This is home, Cassie."

"Yes, Mom, it is now. But that's where I came from."

April had wanted to ignore the comment about the stars, but her gut warned her not to argue. Although Dr. Lucy had offered to have Cassie's DNA analyzed to help determine her father, April had refused and still had no idea who had donated the sperm that produced her child. If Cassie was so sure of coming from the stars, then maybe, maybe those lost weeks had been with someone from the stars. Perhaps that explained the difference in her eyes, her skull formation and her mind that could hold knowledge without limits. Cassie's comment that night had been her first clue, but April wasn't sure she wanted to know.

One late autumn twilight when Cassie was six and April had sent her outside for her daily romp, April read and rocked on the back porch. The sun threw dark shadows from the pines and oaks. Cassie whooped. April dropped the book and stood, awestruck, as a buck, his antlers wide and gleaming, broke across the field, with Cassie, her arms out flung, standing on its back.

She screamed, "Cassie."

She glanced at April and waved.

"It's okay, Mom," she called.

The buck and girl crossed the field, reached the cross fence, and the buck sailed over. Cassie rose above the leaping buck, somersaulted, and landed again with the deer on the other side of the fence.

The twilight silence broke with Cassie's shout as the two of them returned. The buck halted near the back porch and Cassie dropped from its back, patted it on the shoulder, and the buck trotted into the woods.

"Cass, you scared me half to death," April reprimanded her. "Please, don't do that again. You could have been killed if you'd fallen."

"Oh, Mom, I can't fall. And if I do, I can't get hurt."

Her mind had then turned back to the day when as a toddler Cassie had tumbled from the porch to the paving stones at the bottom of the steps. She should have had scrapes and bruises, but she showed no damage to her knees or palms from the fall. And shed no tears but had only grinned when April lifted her.

After her adventure with the buck, she ranged over the farm at will. When April finally realized she was innately knowledgeable about the outdoors, she no longer watched over the youngster like a hen over her biddies.

Cassie brought her observations to April with the excitement of a child and the wisdom of the aged. She told of touching a wild turkey's egg and feeling the heartbeat of the chick inside. She had watched a doe give birth. Watched the fawn as it struggled to his feet and took his first meal. Cassie told her of the thrill to be able to walk up to the wild animals and they showed no fear.

She told her mother her knowledge of life was a gift from the stars.

When Cassie ran to her one afternoon, her voice raised in horror, "Mom, it's Sally. She's hurt. Hurry," April ran to Sally's house. Her friend lay on the floor, blood flowing from her scalp where she had fallen and cut herself on the corner of the coffee table.

"Call 911," she told Cassie. April ran to the bathroom, pulled a clean hand towel from the closet, and pressed it against the cut. The ambulance had to cover 15 miles, and by the time it arrived, Sally was beginning to come around, but was still woozy. The paramedics insisted she go with them, she needed stitches. April assured her she and Cassie would follow and drive her home after the doctors released her.

As they followed the ambulance, April asked Cassie how she knew Sally had fallen.

"Oh, I saw her fall."

"You're supposed to tell me if you leave the yard," April said.

"I didn't leave the yard, Mom."

"Then how did you know?" April stared at her daughter. The car swerved.

"Watch out, Mom!"

April braked, turned her attention back to the road and asked, "Then how did you see her fall?"

Cassie hesitated, gripped the edge of her lower lip in her teeth, and replied, "It's hard to say."

"Well, say it anyhow."

She took a deep breath and released it slowly. "I saw her through the front door."

"What were you doing at her front door?"

"No, Mom, I was in the yard and heard the noise and looked, and saw her on the floor."

"Wait a minute. You heard her fall and went to her front door?"

Cassie fidgeted and shook her head. "Uh… no, I mean I could see her through the door. I was in the yard." She paused and then added. "The door was closed. I could see through it."

"You saw *through* the closed door?"

She swallowed and nodded.

"Can you see through a wall?"

She nodded.

April drew her breath and let it out while staring into the eyes of her child—one iris so pale blue it was almost white and one the rich yellow of spring daffodils. She nodded.

She's got to be a star child. I wonder what else her father's genes have given her? X-ray eyes, 200-plus IQ, photographic memory, visions of home in the stars.

"Okay, sweetheart, but don't tell anyone else you can see through walls. You and I would both be in trouble."

When Cassie was ten, Dr. Lucy suggested she take Cassie to the dentist for a basic evaluation. Cassie had overheard from some of the students at Sunday school mention the horrors of such visits, and objected. April insisted.

The dentist came out to talk to April before Cassie appeared. April asked, "Everything okay?"

He shook his head. "I'm not sure. She already has her wisdom teeth, plus four more. I can't explain why she's got her wisdom teeth in so young, and on top of that, the extra teeth. They are all in excellent condition. Usually girls that age have begun to have some problems from junk food and colas and such."

"We don't do junk food or sodas," she said. "If there's no other problem but good strong teeth and some extras, I guess we're good to go?"

The dentist nodded. "Just be in touch if you need me," shook hands with her, and left. A moment later, Cassie walked out as April paid the bill, her mind on one more difference in her daughter and all other people she knew. *Is she truly a star child?*

Applause interrupted April's thoughts.

On stage, Cassie had finished her introduction and President Jenkins rose, shook hands with the youth, and whispered a suggestion they talk after the ceremonies.

The president stepped to the podium and thanked Cassie for the introduction. The mention of her daughter's name turned April's attention to the president and his speech. He ended with words she remembered from Cassie's speech:

To repeat what your classmate Miss Cassie said to you today:

"When you leave here today, you must decide what road you will take. Will you get in the slow lane and just plod through life? Or the middle lane and speed along and seek more than just an okay living? Or will you hit the fast lane, not the lane to party and pleasure, but the lane that will lead you to higher levels of success than you have dreamed of, the lane that will lead to a future beyond simply walking on the moon, but to beyond, to the stars Only you can decide.

Let's meet somewhere out there in twenty years—somewhere among the stars.

April stood when the President of the United States presented Cassie with her doctorate of philosophy. Others joined her applause and April was pleased that Cassie had made so many friends at MIT.

When the ceremonies finally ended and the president had completed his presidential formalities, April and Cassie joined the president in front of the auditorium. The three were surrounded by secret service men and women as they stood on the sidewalk near the presidential limousine and completed their conversation.

Onlookers were kept behind a police line. Only the agents, Cassie and April were gathered on the sidewalk a few yards from the presidential limo.

Across the street, beyond a line of wooden saw horses and another line of blue-clad local lawmen stood hundreds of presidential supporters. And almost as many presidential haters. Signs read "We love you, Mr. Prez," and almost as many said, "Impeach him."

Sunlight streamed oak shadows across the group. A breeze tickled the leaves. The smell of mud from the Charles River drifted on the wind. In the distance a red shouldered hawk sailed the thermals.

"So what are your plans now, Cassie? You're a bit young for my job, but maybe in a few years. Who knows?"

A shot exploded from the crowd.

Blood spurted from the president's chest.

Cassie lunged at the president.

Two secret service agents grabbed for the president.

A ball of light surrounded Cassie and the fallen president.

The two agents jumped away, their hands singed by the light.

An agent shoved April to the ground.

Another agent dashed across the street in pursuit of the shooter.

The thousand-odd onlookers fled.

The shooter disappeared with the crowd.

The ball of light disappeared, Cassie stood up and pulled the president to his feet. A patch of blood showed on the president's jacket and on the concrete at his feet.

"He's okay," Cassie yelled.

Two agents grabbed Cassie. She shrugged herself free, leaving the agents holding her robe. Beneath it, she had worn jeans and a cotton shirt and tennis shoes. She darted across the street, through the fleeing crowd, and passed the agent who stood looking for the shooter.

Within seconds, Cassie returned, pushing the shooter. On one finger of her other hand she held the assassin's .357 magnum long-barrel pistol by the trigger guard. She stopped in front of one of the agents.

"Here's your shooter," she said. "And his weapon."

Cassis trotted to April while President Jenkins brushed dried blood from his jacket and wondered what had happened as two members of his protection detail tried to shove him into the presidential limousine.

So began the journey of Cassiopeia, the Star Child, into mythology as the Supreme Heroine of America, while unknown to her or April, Cassie had a half-brother in Montana, a cowboy who at fourteen was having the time of his life as an acrobatic performer at rodeos, and as a student he amazed professors at the University with his knowledge of the stars.

EXIT LAUGHING
The Flower of the Fleet

He had been arrogant when he left Annapolis and arrogance seemed to fit him perfectly. It grew with him as he gained rank. Somehow he managed to kowtow just enough to those in higher rank to not only maintain his rank but to earn promotions. His fitness reports did not reflect that he expected to be treated as "His Lordship" by those who served under him.

Although he bore only slight symptoms, when he tested positive for Covid-19, he immediately had his ship-board physician refer him to the base hospital. The physician was protecting the shipboard crew; the captain was ensuring that he would be first in line for any medical help available.

From seaman recruit to master chief, the enlisted personnel knew about his Lordship, but he expected to be addressed name and rank in full when underlings greeted him. Most kept a straight face through the greetings and salutes— "Good Morning, Captain Bly"—but snickered when they were out of sight. Most wished him a worse fate than the other Captain Bligh. Their Captain Bly had fewer letters in his name, they said, but he made up for them with arrogance.

When he arrived at the Covid-19 ward, he was offered a bed in the ward with the other infected sailors and officers.

Nurse Nancy, a commander, was in charge of that wing of the infec-tious diseases ward. Officers and enlisted lay in bunks alongside each wall.

"You do realize I am a captain. I need my own private room." He lifted his briefcase. "I will have to work while I am confined here."

"Yes, sir, right away," she replied and led him into the hall and to the patient room immediately off the ward. "I hope this is suitable. It's the only private space we have on this wing, and since your diagnosis is Covid-19, you are going to be with us for the duration."

She pointed out his face mask which lay on the pillow, and explained procedures. She ended by instructing him to don the hospital gown and she went to tend to other patients. She closed the door so he would have the privacy he demanded.

She had barely reached the ward when Captain Bly bellowed for more water. She complied, and as she backed out of his door again, the entire ward heard her "I'm sorry, Captain, but you won't be checking out to the Officers' Club from this ward, and I would be refused entrance because of my assignment on this ward."

So different from the lads in the sick ward. Sick as some of them had been, they had all managed to treat her like a sister. Grateful she had not lost a patient, she could only smile and tease them back. Hers was the only ward designated for treating Covid-19, but her patients' optimism and camaraderie infused her with hope for each. Their illness ignored rank and endowed equality. They turned their backs on the possibility of dying.

Every evening when she began her last rounds before heading to her own quarters, they chanted: "Corona, Corona, we want our Corona."

At first, she simply shook her head and waved. She had finally gone off station and found a poster advertising the beer. It now decorated one wall.

Nurse Commander Nancy was grateful to see the end of her shift when others would have the fun of dealing with Captain Bly. As she walked into the ward for the last check on her patients and they began to chant, Captain Bly roared, "Quiet! This is a hospital!"

Nurse Nancy raised both hands, palms toward her guys and patted the air. "Sorry, men. I'll think of something."

The next day was worse. If she walked by his door on the way to the nurses' station, he yelled "Oh, Nurse..." and demanded fresh water or some crackers, or complained the sheets were hot and needed to be changed, or when was the next meal or couldn't she get a steward's mate to come take his uniform to the cleaners. His invitations to her to go to the Officers' Club with him for supper and drinks was overheard by some of the sailors in sick bay and repeated and expanded.

The attending nurses and aides and the tended-to began to despise Bly with the same intensity as his shipboard subordinates did.

When she returned to duty the next morning, she noticed an addition to the schedule: Admiral's Inspection.

Her first thought was *Salvation. Now to figure out how to use it to advantage.*

She announced the event to the crew in the ward and then informed the captain his supervisor would be by to have a look-see at his sickroom. Bly assured her he would be glad to have the room squared away; he could work on his computer while a medic cleaned up.

The Admiral was due on board at 1300 hours. At 1245, Nurse

Nancy entered Captain Bly's room, thermometer in hand, and told him she needed to take his temperature. He opened his mouth. "No, no. You need your mask on. Have to protect anyone who comes by. Put it on now. So this has to be rectal." She handed him his face mask and when it was in place, she said, "Please hop in the bunk, sir."

He did and at her instructions rolled onto his belly. She walked around the bed so she faced the door. He turned his head toward her. She flipped the hospital gown up to expose his butt.

He stoically did not flinch when he felt the cold tube slide into his rectum.

"Just hold still. Whatever you do, don't move or you may dislodge the thermometer. I'll be right back," Nurse Nancy commanded. She left the door standing wide open when she left.

Moments later, all the men in the ward glided in single file from the ward door into the hall, each man clad in the hospital gown designed by Dr. C. Moore Butts. No one had any interest in the half-bare butt in front of him; all were interested, however, in the bare butt of the *butt* in the private room.

Hospital slippers whispered to the floor as they began to pass by, each one pausing as he reached the door, just long enough to click his cell phone camera. Hands covered mouths already covered with masks in an attempt to suppress snickers.

Captain Bly called, "Nurse! Oh nurse."

Nurse Nancy did not appear. Instead a male nurse with a face mask and plastic shield entered, strode around the bed to face him, and asked, "You need something, Captain?"

"What's all that noise out there? I'm not supposed to move or turn over. Are we evacuating?"

"Oh, no sir. It's just the patients in the ward going to the mess hall. Doctor said it would be good for them to get some exercise. Most will be discharged by the end of the week."

"Are they taking pictures? Light has been bouncing off the wall here."

"Well, one of the men has fallen in love with Nurse Nancy and every time they get close together someone wants to take a picture. Afraid it won't be a match made in the chapel, though. Sailor is a seaman and nineteen." The nurse chuckled and walked out. He left the door wide open.

The noises outside suddenly went from soft shuffles to quiet scurrying as the sailors rushed back to their own bedside positions for the Admiral's inspection.

Admiral Wilson's voice preceded him down the hallway as he spoke with his aide. "I understand our good Captain Bly is here, under observation for the virus. "

"Yes sir. In the private room here."

Footsteps stopped at the door.

Wilson's shouted, "Bly, what in hell are you doing?"

Bly raised up onto his elbows and turned his head to look at the admiral. "I'm just having my temperature taken. Haven't you seen someone get a rectal temperature?"

The admiral's voice rolled down the hall and across the ward. "My God, man. Yeah. But never with a daffodil."

Laughter rolling from the ward drowned out the clatter as Captain Bly scrambled from the bed, knocked over the bedside tray-table, his computer, his water jug and glass, and an open bottle of Corona beer as he struggled to remove the flower blooming from his butt.

www.ingramcontent.com/pod-product-compliance
Lightning Source LLC
Chambersburg PA
CBHW031836170626
46807CB00004B/1492